I0784466

BAH HOMBURG!

Bonnie Cavaliere

Mind's Eye Media, Incorporated

eBook ISBN: 979-8-9857928-8-1

Print ISBN: 979-8-9857928-7-4

Mind's Eye Media, Incorporated

United States of America

CONTENTS

A Merry Band

I DON'T GET SEASICK. Mostly because I'm smart enough to take Bonine about an hour before I step aboard any boat. However, several of my cast mates were looking a little green. The small ferry that was taking us from the tip of Pine Island to Nokosi Island was having a rough time in the choppy waters of the not-so-serene Gulf of Mexico. I turned my head as Laura, our stage manager, leaned over the side of the boat. I had already checked wind direction and had shifted my position accordingly. Our fearless leader, Josh, looked away quickly. He and Laura were an item, but it didn't look like he would be much help to her. In fact, I figured he might be the next to blow. I'm not proud, but that made me a little happy.

I'm Kasey McCormick, standup comedian and for the holiday season, Carol, a friendly elf in a fairly funny spoof of *A Christmas Carol*. (Yes! I got the title role! My parents are so proud. Of course, they have no idea what a low-rent production this is.) Outside of my stand-up comedy routine, it was the first piece I had written that had been performed. Josh pronounced it "mildly funny" and "good enough" for the audiences we would have.

Our cast was on its way to a private corporate party on a very private island and it promised to be swanky. You can only reach the island by boat or helicopter and you better have an invitation when you show up. In normal circumstances, none of us would be allowed anywhere near this place. But here we were. Or almost were, if the cast could make the crossing without dying.

They had carpooled down from Tampa to the Fort Myers area in a mini-van. I drove myself, mostly because I don't like to depend on other people, whether it's for a ride or anything else. We left the vehicles in the marina parking lot and bundled ourselves and our gear onto the small boat. *A Comedy Christmas Carol* was a show that required little in the way of costumes and props and since we were responsible for our own costumes, the only big items were the prop trunk and a portable sound system, which Herbie, the sound guy, had thought to double-wrap in plastic garbage bags.

The boat could carry about twenty people. There were six of us and we were the only passengers. The guests were probably already on island. We were the evening's entertainment for a four-day corporate holiday party. I had never worked for a company that had four-day parties for their employees. Josh had quickly corrected me when I mentioned it at one of our rehearsals.

"It's not for the employees. This is executives only. And spouses. The little people get a three-hour buffet with dancing at the Holiday Inn," Josh explained, with more than a touch of condescension in his voice.

He went on to lecture us on the fact that we were not guests, we were workers and even though we would be staying over at the hotel, we were not to mingle as equals. *Well, pardon me*, I thought. *I'll try not to fart.*

"It's a Meet and Greet after the show. That means we're polite, we're on our best behavior, and we do not get drunk."

"No drinking?" This came from Herbie, but Dan and Colin, aka Elf 1 and Elf 2, looked unhappy, too.

"Not at the party. We do the show, they'll give us something to eat and you can have a drink then. A DRINK. One."

Herbie shrugged.

"And no smoking dope, either." Josh glared at him.

"Not a problem. I'm a professional, man." Herbie rolled his eyes before pretending to check his equipment.

I'M NOT A BIG drinker, but I don't like being told what I can and can't do. Or more to the point, being treated like a child. Josh had a nasty streak. He is the reason why the stereotype of "short man syndrome" exists. He was about five foot seven, and I made sure to always wear heels around him. I towered over him, even in low heels.

Most of the cast and crew had been the object of some derisive comment from him at one time or another. He tried it once on me. I very quietly told him if he ever used that tone with me again, I'd pull myself and my script out from under him. I learned a long time ago that most bullies fold the minute someone confronted them. I have four brothers; I'm not big on taking crap from anybody.

Which is why I had a nice bottle of single malt scotch tucked away in my bag. It was secured in bubble wrap and a big Ziploc, but I was keeping an eye on my bag in case things went sliding. I also had my road/room food in there. I never go anywhere without provisions. Who knows? I could slide off the highway and not be found for a week. Which is why I also had a one-pound bag of Twizzlers, chocolate stuffed Oreos, Kettlicious Kettle Corn (I ate a quarter of a very large bag on the way down), a Peppermint Patty, and two Lindt dark chocolate bars. All of it precious cargo. I did not want it to go sliding into the water.

The Gulf of Mexico is normally pretty tame, but the water gets a tad bit colder and rougher in the winter and a storm had kicked up the waves and wind. Purplish-grey clouds, fat with rain, threatened overhead. I hoped they would hold off until we had ourselves and the equipment inside. The boat bounced in the chop and the bow slapped down arhythmically. I mentally patted myself on the back for taking the seasickness pills.

The trip was nearly done. I could see the landing and above it, what looked to be a large hotel. I was glad I didn't have a lot to carry. We were just there overnight. We'd set up this afternoon, do the show tonight, leave at noon tomorrow. We were each getting $200 for the show, food and accommodations thrown into the deal. I figured Josh was getting a much bigger cut than the rest of us, but then, he was producer and director. Plus, he had booked us the gig. I was fine with the money. I was fine with the not drinking in front of the customers. I was thrilled that my little show was being produced. I made sure Josh didn't know that.

Not Quite Fantasy Island

THERE WERE SEVERAL GOLF carts waiting to take us from the ferry landing to the hotel. No cars were allowed on the island; yachts and private helicopters were welcome though. The little marina was filled with expensive boats, not one of which looked rundown, and all were battened down, the excess lines coiled Bristol fashion. The dock master had come out to help the ferry captain tie up. The two worked together smoothly and the gangway was dropped within minutes. The two helped us out of the boat and onto the pier.

Laura groaned as she put her feet on dry land, and swayed a bit. Herbie steadied her.

"I'll check us in," Josh said, ignoring Laura, taking the first cart and leaving the rest of us to bring up the prop trunk and sound equipment. Laura seemed to not notice that her boyfriend hadn't given her a second thought.

"It's good to be the king," Colin muttered under his breath. I had my hands full with my bag and my computer case. I shouldered them both and helped him with the prop trunk. Laura and Dan were helping Herbie hump the sound equipment to the second cart. We loaded the prop trunk onto the third cart. With all the equipment, there wasn't room for everyone.

Laura was normally practical and efficient, but I could tell she had not recovered from the ride over. I figured the sooner she got to a bathroom, the better.

"Why don't you three ride up with the equipment and Colin and I will wait here for the next cart."

Herbie and Laura rode with the props trunk. Dan was tall—around six foot, four inches, and he sat on the back of the sound equipment cart. He had his feet on the bumper which basically put his knees up to his chin.

We watched them drive soundlessly up the rise to the hotel. I looked at Colin. The wind was blowing his wild red curls across his face and he carelessly brushed the hair out of his eyes. "I should have tied it back. You were smart."

"I didn't know if it would be an open boat or not. Glad there was some cover. It's freaking freezing."

It wasn't, of course. But anything under 70 degrees is freezing to Floridians and it was probably only about 60 today. And damp. I had a sweatshirt on under my windbreaker. Sure, I can take the cold weather; I come from hearty New England stock. I just don't choose to.

We watched a cart trail down the drive. It made a little whirring sound as it pulled up and the driver jumped out to help us with our bags. We climbed in and the cart smoothly started up.

"Just like Disney World," Colin said.

I nodded. In less than two minutes we were deposited at the front of the hotel and the driver grabbed our bags. I opted to carry my computer case and noticed Colin did the same thing.

"You brought yours, too?" I asked.

"I live on it. I figured we'll have dead time between set up this afternoon and the show, and then time tonight. I suspect there's not a lot to do here if you're not a guest."

I agreed. I liked Colin. He had good timing, knew his lines, and wasn't a prima donna. But I didn't think of him as someone who planned ahead for anything. Maybe I didn't know enough about acting, but it seemed to me that most people were typecast. If you could sing and dance and were pretty, you were the ingénue. If you could sing and dance and weren't pretty, you were the best friend and/or comic relief. There's a reason why every TV sitcom has a wacky neighbor.

Our cast was no different. Dan was young, handsome, and destined to play the romantic lead. He was a natural for rom-coms. Colin, thirty-ish with his wild red curls, black-framed glasses, and somewhat ordinary looks, would always be cast as the comic relief. He looked a bit like a mad scientist, which made him perfect as Elf #3. I was passably pretty, couldn't dance and can barely carry a tune, but I know how to deliver a line. Standup comedy trains you for that. You learn to use pauses, silences, long looks (called takes) to the audience to milk out a laugh. I've also learned the value of my native Boston accent. I sound like everyone else from Massachusetts, but in most areas of the country, it is different enough to get a laugh. In fact, I had trained the accent out of me when I was fifteen. I did open mics for over a year without the accent. Then I worked with a Boston comic one weekend and naturally fell back into the rhythm. I did my set in my real accent and got more laughs than ever before. The accent stayed. At least on stage.

Truth be told, the accent was why I was working with Josh in the first place. He had a dinner theatre show with a character from Boston. Very few actors on the Gulf Coast of Florida do a Boston accent; everyone does New York, thinking they're doing Boston. Josh, for all his flaws, knew the difference. I walked in with the real thing and was immediately cast in that show. It was nice work but the show wasn't pulling like it used to. Josh's business fell off during the Christmas season. People wanted a holiday show, something fast for parties that wouldn't be too expensive. I sat down and wrote a parody of Dickens' *A Christmas Carol*. Small cast, no set, with a forty-five-minute run time. I even put in audience interaction, which was Josh's big thing. It was a winner. And, since it was my show, I wrote the starring role for me.

This was our fourth or fifth time doing the show for an audience. Dan, Colin, and I were comfortable working together, we knew our lines and all we really needed to do was check out where we would be doing the show—a banquet room, as it turned out. The guests would have cocktails and hors d'oeuvres, we'd do our show, they'd go eat an over-priced dinner. Then the night was ours. We would get dinner in the staff dining area. Which was a nice way of saying we weren't allowed to mingle with the guests. That was fine by me. I had no problem being holed up in my room watching TV. But I was glad I brought my bottle.

Josh was in the lobby, trying to look like he belonged and failing miserably. If he had been at all pleasant, he might have passed for the concierge. He handed out keys to the rooms which were conveniently all on the same hall.

"Everybody drop your things in your rooms and be back down here in 15 minutes. We need to get the room set up for the show. Fifteen minutes people. And don't be late." Josh had a way of accusing people of doing things before they could have possibly done them.

Dan nodded his head earnestly. I could tell he was already getting nerved up, working into his "character." Laura and Herbie took the prop trunk and sound equipment on a dolly to the banquet room, while Josh followed behind them, issuing orders. Dan, Colin and I grabbed our bags and crowded onto the elevator.

"The glamor of show business," Colin said.

"I'm hoping they give us a decent meal." A decent meal to me is something I'll actually eat. I'm a picky eater and when what I eat is in someone else's hands, I like to have back up. No food and I get hangry—hungry and angry. It's not pretty. Which is another reason why I travel with a lot of road food. I don't like to be either.

"Wonder if they have a full bar or just beer and wine," Dan said.

"Full bar." Colin sounded certain.

"Have you been here before?"

He hesitated for a second. "No, it's just that a place like this would need to carry just about everything and most of it will be top shelf. I've bartended in my day." That made sense. "I brought my own top shelf."

"Me, too. Scotch."

Colin laughed. "Bourbon."

Dan looked a little lost. "I didn't know we could bring our own."

"Well, Dan," Colin explained. "No one said we couldn't."

"Don't worry. We'll share."

The elevator doors opened up and we looked at our room key envelopes for the numbers and followed the arrow to the left. Colin and Dan were next to each other. I was across from Dan.

"Remember, kids. Fifteen minutes. Don't be late," Dan did a perfect imitation of Josh. We all laughed and headed into our rooms.

My room was pretty standard. Two queen size beds, which is standard. Huge flat screen TV, mini-fridge, mini-bar, microwave. All of it very nice, don't get me wrong. I put my bag on the luggage stand and quickly hung up my costume and the change of clothes I brought. I had a dress for the Meet and Greet but I had a bad feeling we would be doing it in costume. Just another way to let us know we were the help.

I grabbed my toiletry bag (okay, it's a Ziploc baggie) and brought it into the bathroom.

"Oh. Wow."

Now I knew why they charged so much to stay at this place. The bathroom was almost as large as the main room. There was a double sink, lighted makeup mirror, heated towel rack, hair dryer, drawers to put things in, and plenty of counter space. But the centerpiece of the room was an eight-foot bathtub (separate from the huge shower stall) with Jacuzzi jets. A 42" TV was positioned high up on the wall so you could relax in the tub and watch TV while you soaked. Suddenly, being stuck in a hotel room was not such a bad thing.

I tucked my things away, brushed my teeth, and headed back down to the lobby. Better to be a little early than late. Besides, I could check to see what the gift shop carried in case my food supply ran low. I was hoping for Häagen-Dazs ice cream bars.

I was the first one down so I explored. The gift shop was to the right of the front desk. I poked my head in there first, checked to see how late it was open, and was glad to see three different types of ice cream, including Häagen-Dazs bars. There were also crackers and cheese, a good supply of candy, and they even carried beer and wine. The prices were outrageous, of course. But the ice cream was in my budget. I'd be back.

I crossed back through the lobby and followed the signs to the workout room and indoor pool. I most likely wouldn't be hitting either. The glass in the pool area was steamy and the smell of chlorine permeated the hall. I doubled-back to the lobby and found Dan and Colin.

"Well, we're on time. Where's Josh?" Dan asked.

"He doesn't need to be on time," Colin replied. "He's the di-rec-tor."

"And the rules do not apply to the di-rec-tor," I finished.

"He's probably in the event room, setting up."

I nodded. "Well, we might as well head that way since that's where we're going to end up."

Dan was looking around, taking everything in. He looked at me uncertainly.

"Do you have a nice bathtub?"

"Oh, yeah. It's like a swimming pool."

"There's a tub *and* a shower stall."

"Yes."

"That's pretty nice."

"Yes."

"I've never stayed anywhere this nice."

"It's just a hotel room, Dan."

"But, what if I break something? I can't afford to replace anything in that room. Even the sheets feel like they're expensive. I bet they cost a hundred bucks at least."

Crap. He was getting freaked out.

"Oh, no. They get them at bulk rates. They probably lose more sheets a week than you have bought in your lifetime. I'm thinking they pay like twenty bucks for each set."

"Oh. Well, sure." I watched him take a breath and nod to himself.

"But don't go into the mini-bar. It'll set you back a few hundred," Colin kidded.

Dan's eyes grew wide. "I had a pack of almonds. How much do you think those were?"

"Nuts? Probably not much," Colin said. "Twenty, thirty bucks tops."

Dan's head snapped around. "Twenty dollars??"

"He's kidding." I shot a look of admonishment at Colin. "They're about six. There's a little sign that tells you the prices."

"I don't like this place. I don't belong here."

"You will. It just takes getting used to."

Colin chimed in. "When you're a famous actor, you won't look twice at the prices. You'll open all the mini-bar food and only eat half of it."

"In the meantime, I think it would be a good acting exercise to work on a character who would feel comfortable here. Someone who was born into money and this is just normal, everyday stuff for them."

Dan brightened. "Yeah. That could be fun."

We could hear Josh's voice coming from one of the rooms, testing the sound. There was no need for him to do that; we would run the sound check and Herbie needed to adjust the mics to our voices, not his. Josh just liked to have his fingers in every little thing.

"Into the breach," said Colin. He opened the door and ushered us in with a bow.

The room was set with about 10 round tables, six chairs at each in a semi-circle facing the area where we would be performing. At least we wouldn't have people's backs to us. There were two portable bars set in the back of the room on either side. We did the run-through without a hitch, though Josh made sure he seemed displeased with it. God forbid we should make him happy. It was a manipulation. I was old enough to recognize it as was Colin. Dan was still intimidated by it. He'd learn.

THERE'S NO DIGNITY IN *comedy*, I reminded myself, looking in the mirror and applying still more red blush in big circles on my cheeks. I was wearing a green polyester tunic mini-dress, with red trim and a red belt, candy-cane striped stockings and green elf slippers with jingle bells. The hat was green with red trim and we had added extra bells for comic effect. At least the green looked great with my red hair. I was adorable. I snarled at my image in the mirror.

I gathered up my show bag—hair brush, makeup, mini sewing kit, scissors, tape. I threw a coat on over my costume and carried my elf hat, but there was no disguising the elf booties with jingle bells on them.

I waited for the elevator, hoping it would be empty. No such luck. A well-dressed, middle-aged couple moved aside as the doors opened. I got in, jingling musically with each step. The elevator smelled of expensive perfume and possibly gin.

"Are you one of the performers?"

I pretended confusion. "What gave me away?"

She laughed. "Oh, you're so funny! Isn't she funny, Edward?"

"Very droll, Irene."

She leaned into me. "You're very funny."

Which is when I realized she was very drunk. Hoo boy. This was going to be a show.

"Thank you. I hope you're sitting down front tonight."

"Oh, we will be! I was going to be an actress, you know. But then I met Edward."

"Well, from one actress to another, I think you made a wiser choice than I did."

She hooted with laughter. Edward shifted his weight from one foot to the other but he didn't look displeased.

"You're a little early for the show," I ventured.

"Yes, but we're fashionably late for the cocktail hour." She winked at me. "I can only make so much small talk with the juniors' wives. Or our hostess, for that matter."

"Irene," Edward's voice was sharp.

"Oh, please Edward. Everyone knows Marie Janeé is a climber."

"Yes, but she has climbed into the boss's bed, so make nice, Irene."

I realized Edward had downed a few pops himself. Their mini-bar bill was going to be substantial.

"Well, I have to put up with Mrs. Claus. She's started making gluten-free cookies and we all have to pretend they taste good." I rolled my eyes dramatically. "The boss's wife. Eeeesh. Life was so much better before Santa had his cholesterol checked."

We were laughing as the elevator doors opened to the lobby and heads turned.

"See you inside," Irene said cheerfully. And really, if you thought about it, she was full of cheer.

I left them at the banquet room door and continued down the hallway to the makeshift Green Room. Laura was already there, fussing with the props. Her blond hair was pulled back and she was dressed in black pants and a black turtleneck, typical backstage attire in a theatre. I wasn't sure it was necessary since we didn't really have a stage, or an offstage, or a real backstage. But Laura liked to do things properly and it did give us a more theatrical air.

"You know, they say women are always late, but that's not what I'm seeing."

She smiled. "Josh takes more time than I do getting ready. His hair has to be brushed just so. I think he brought three different jackets to wear tonight. I had to talk him out of bringing his tuxedo."

"A little over the top."

"Whereas I'm going to have to do a quick change after the show." She indicated a plastic dry cleaner bag with what looked like two dresses in it. Josh wasn't the only one who had a hard time deciding what to wear. "Which one do you think?" She flipped the bag around so I could see the other dress.

"Definitely the red. It's a holiday party."

"They're both red!"

"I mean the brighter red with the spaghetti straps. The burgundy one is pretty, but the other one is more partyish."

She nodded.

"We'll be busy with the Meet and Greet. You'll have time to change."

The door swung open and Dan and Colin came in. They were wearing the same red and white candy-cane striped tights I was, with matching elf shoes. Colin had opted for an elf costume that had knickers but we couldn't find a second one in Dan's size. The only costume we found that would fit him was a tunic that was dangerously short. Josh had supplied him with a dancer's cup, but it was still—shall we say—not a good look. We tried to make sure he didn't raise his arms over his head, which lifted up the whole tunic, but sometimes he forgot. Colin and I had become very quick at jumping in front of him. By the third show, it had become a running gag.

We were stowing our gear when Josh came in, escorting a well-dressed couple. The man was tall, in what must have been a hand-tailored suit. The shoes were definitely handmade. Italian. I know shoes. Marie Janeé was petite and perfect. Blond and blue-eyed, straight nose with just a bit of an upturn, and lips that had obviously been botoxed. She was wearing a strapless, Christmas-red, beaded cocktail dress that could not have been bought in Florida, unless she had been down to Worth Avenue in West Palm recently. It clung to her body perfectly, accenting her generous bustline. Even in four-inch heels, she was short.

"You've met Laura, of course. I'd like to introduce you to your castmates this evening."

He introduced us as Carol, Elf One and Elf Two. It was his little way of letting us know that we were the help. I have my insecurities, but Josh had a whole 'nother level going on.

"Cast, this is Stephen Vashon, founder and CEO of VashTech, and his lovely wife, Marie Janeé. Mr. Vashon will be your Scrooge this evening."

We shook hands. Dan, always the first to step in it, said, "So have you done any acting before?"

Stephen gave a short laugh. "Ah, no. Except occasionally pretending the company was doing well in spite of a rough patch. But that's been a while."

"Don't worry, sir. We'll take good care of you. Nothing employees like to see better than a boss who can make a bit of fun at himself." I looked over at Marie Janeé. "Your job is to enjoy yourself."

"I always enjoy myself," she said. It sounded just a bit condescending and she gave me a look that was definitely territorial. Really? I was dressed like an elf. Pretty sure I was not looking like any sort of competition to her. She shifted moods easily. "It will be fun to see if Stephen has any acting chops."

"Marie Janeé and I worked in, um, regional theatre together," Josh put in.

"A long time ago," she laughed, but it rang false. She obviously wanted to put that life behind her. And judging from the rock on her finger and the rest of the jewelry collection she had draped over various body parts, she had.

That old connection explained how Josh had landed this gig. We had done some corporate gigs, but this was by far the swankiest.

Josh was falling all over himself explaining how the evening would go and what Stephen would be doing. Laura was standing politely at Josh's elbow, but it was as if she didn't exist. Colin looked over at me and raised an eyebrow. I gave just a trace of a head shake back. Josh was trying way too hard. The trick to sucking up was not to be obvious about it. Marie Janeé looked around the room as if she were smelling dog poop.

"And there will be cue cards for your lines. Laura, show Mr. Vashon the cue cards."

Laura went to the props table and picked one up. "I'll be in a spot where you can see me easily. No need for glasses." She smiled at him reassuringly.

"Also, we tend to throw this hat back and forth." Dan held up a homburg hat, then twirled it on his finger. It made a jingling sound as it spun. It had been Herbie's idea to attach jingle bells inside the hat. It made for an extra bit of fun. We'd all gotten very clever with the hat.

Dan gave the hat a little toss. "So, when you see it go flying by, you say 'Bah homburg!' There's no cue card for that."

Mr. Vashon smiled at him, clearly up for the kitsch. "I'll do my best."

"One more thing," I said. I held up a candy cane striped sleeping cap.

"I have to wear that." It was a statement. This was sometimes the sticking point with our Scrooges. Which is why I had the job of telling them.

"It will get a big laugh, I promise."

He looked at me uncertainly, then shrugged. "In for a penny." He was a sport.

The good thing about working with senior level people was that they were used to being in front of people and giving talks. I had no doubt Mr. Vashon would be just fine, which made our job easier.

Josh took over again. "So, we'll get started in about ten minutes. I'll come out and do a short introduction, thank you and Marie Janeé, and bring out the cast. Carol will pick you out of the audience as if she doesn't know who you are, which always gets a big laugh. The show runs about forty-five minutes, we'll end with a quick sing-along of "We Wish You a Merry Christmas..." he paused here. "Is that okay or do you want something secular?"

"I think it fits with the Dickens theme," Stephen said smoothly. I had to hand it to him, the guy was all-in.

"We'll end with a quick sing-along, then we have a fifteen-minute meet-and-mingle with the cast, and then, on to dinner."

"Sounds great. I'm sure my people will enjoy the show. He turned to us. "Looking forward to working with you."

We responded in kind. As they turned to go, I heard Marie Janeé say to Josh, "Your assistant does know that dinner is semi-formal, right? She'll be changing."

"Oh, of course."

I saw Laura blushing furiously. She turned away and busied herself with the props table. The door closed behind them and I went over to get my props.

"So, she's a piece of work."

"I hate that Josh introduces me as his assistant. We've been going out for over a year."

"I think he just wants to make the business look more professional."

"Or maybe he wants to look single to his old girlfriend."

"They dated?"

"What do you think?"

"Maybe. They could just have been friends. But let's face it, Josh can't compete with Stephen Vashon. Did you see the ring?"

Laura's eyes widened. "Oh my God! You couldn't miss it. It was blinding."

Colin had come up behind us. "Couldn't miss the boob job, either."

"I was not going to go there, but now that you have..."

We all laughed.

"We'll do the show, say our hellos, you will sit through a fabulous dinner, and tomorrow, we will leave this all behind us. Just another show."

Laura nodded, but I could tell Marie Janeé had upset her. Or maybe it was Josh. Or both.

Josh came back in. "Five minutes everyone. Places. This is an important gig. It could lead to more throughout the year. So, don't blow it. Let's give them a great show."

Somehow Josh's pre-show pep talks were never inspiring. Dan and Colin collected their props. Laura took the cue cards and the hats. She had pre-set the few props that we would grab from a side table during the show. There was never any real backstage at these events.

We waited at the door that connected our "Green Room" such as it was to the event room. We heard Josh make the introduction, then the music came up, and in we went.

Last Dance with Marie Janeé

The show was going well. The guests were in high spirits (literally) and they were happy to engage. We pulled Stephen into the show as Scrooge, which of course delighted everyone. We chose different audience members for each of the ghosts in turn and it seemed like each choice was a direct hit. The minute we pulled someone from the audience, the guests responded with clapping and laughter and for Ghost #2, a big "Whoaah!" I figured we had pulled a real muckety-muck on that one. What was nice was that everyone was a good sport and didn't need a lot of coaxing. We would whisper the lines to the "ghosts" and they would say them and it was so kitschy that everyone just played along.

Some days, my job is really fun. This was one of them. The script was filled with bad puns and cultural references and of course, you couldn't mention Tiny Tim without giving a nod to the ukulele strumming Tiny Tim of the 80s. I was surprised that people still got the reference, but they did. We were wrapping the show.

Me, as Carol: "He ordered the biggest turkey in town."

Dan: "Gilbert Gottfried?"

Me, pretending to be exasperated: "NO! A tom turkey!"

Colin (sweetly): "Awww. A tom for Tim."

I continued: "The largest turkey he could find to be delivered to the Cratchit house. Then he hurried off to celebrate Christmas with his own family, shouting the words of Tiny Tim…"

We had the CEO standing with us and had given him the cue card to hold up, which he did.

Me: "Help us out…"

And the audience chorused "God bless us every one!" I love when an audience gets into it. Seriously, it's incredibly rewarding as a performer.

Me: "That always makes me cry."

Dan: "Really? Cause Hallmark commercials always make me cry."

Colin: "Well, the Bucs make me cry."

We waited for the predicted laugh and got it. Even when they had Tom Brady, the Bucs had their ups and downs.

I continued, "Well, we've got a lot of work to do. Remember that naughty and nice survey?" I paused and nodded at them as a warning to be nice. "Let the story of Scrooge serve as a reminder…"

Colin, Dan and I said the line together: "Don't give fruitcake for Christmas!"

We closed out the show with a short medley of holiday songs and had everybody singing with us. We took one last bow and disappeared (as the help does) out a side door into our make-shift Green Room. There would be a fifteen-minute break between the show and their dinner being served where we were supposed to mingle and make nice, but stay in character. It gave people time to get another drink, go to the restrooms if need be, or whatever. After that, we were done for the night and expected to disappear. I was more than happy to do so. Josh and Laura were invited to the official dinner. The rest of us would go to the staff dining room.

We waited in the Green Room for a couple of minutes and then went back into the main room. People had, for the most part, left their seats and were moving around—back to the cocktail party atmosphere. The Meet and Greet was fairly typical, shaking hands, exchanging pleasantries and accepting the usual compliments. We split up and worked the room quickly. Staying in character, we made a fuss over the people we had pulled out of the audience, thanking them for being such good sports. I must have agreed that yes, 'Stephen was quite good' a dozen times. "He could probably go into acting if this CEO gig doesn't work out," was becoming my standard line. I tried not to say it while standing too close to the last group I had told that joke to. Then I overheard some guy I had talked to say it to his group and get a laugh. He probably stole his subordinates' ideas and pitched them as his own in meetings. At that point, the line was dead for me. I got over myself, moved on to another group and made nice. It wasn't like I got paid extra for coming up with good cocktail small talk.

My stomach was having a hard time ignoring the trays of hors d'oeuvres that were being passed around. The staff kept offering them to us and we had to refuse. ("GUESTS ONLY!" Josh had reminded us.) Frosted my butt, too. I like those little mini-quiche things. Just one wouldn't hurt. I didn't see Laura, but Josh was still in the room. No joy for Christmas Carol. I looked around for a clock, but this banquet room was like Vegas: Management didn't want people to track how much time had passed. I'd been circulating long enough to have done my job and I figured our requisite fifteen minutes were just about up. I tried to catch Dan's eye, but he was chatting up the trophy wife of one of the executives. Not smart. But it was a testimony to how good-looking Dan was, even in that ridiculous costume. I was about to butt in on the conversation when I saw Colin heading over to him. Sometimes we rescue Dan from women, sometimes we rescue him from himself. I suspected this was a case of the latter. I saw them looking towards the door to the Green Room and I was about to catch up to them and suggest we disappear, when I got hugged from the side.

"Christmas Carol!" It was Edward from the elevator. Apparently, he had caught up to Irene's level of inebriation. "You were fantastic." The side hug was turning into a not-so-subtle boob-feel. I shifted away.

"Did you enjoy the show?"

"Very much. I'd love to talk to you about maybe doing a show for our family party. Maybe we could meet after dinner?"

"That would be great, but you will need to talk with Josh about that. He's our producer. I am but a lowly elf."

Colin came up and rescued me. It was kind of an unwritten rule that we watched out for each other during shows as well as Meet and Greets. All of the shows our troupe did were heavy on audience participation and some members of the audience took that as license to come on to us, or worse. Once someone punched my fake pregnancy belly during one of the wedding shows we did. I guess he was checking to see if it was real, but you have to wonder about a guy who thought it was just fine to land a full punch on a woman, fake belly or not. For the record, six inches of pillow does not do much to block a punch. Put a few drinks in people and you had no idea what they would do.

We made our excuses, grabbed Dan, and headed back to the Green Room. I was pissed and needed to be away from the guests. It just takes one asshole to ruin what would have been such a fun memory.

Laura had changed into the red cocktail dress for dinner. "I hate to ask, but..." She indicated the props.

"No problem. They haven't gone into dinner yet. Go get yourself a drink," Colin said.

"And have one of those mini-quiches for me." I was perhaps more miffed about that than Edward's groping.

It took less than five minutes to repack the props trunk. Laura had already put the two hats into their special hat boxes, Marley's cape was on a hanger next to them. I felt bad for Herbie, still working in the event room. He had to wait for it to clear before he could turn off the background music and start packing up.

Dan and Colin left and I put my small collection of things back into my show bag. I headed toward the elevators, only to find myself at the side hall to the workout room. Wrong way. I glanced down that way and got more than I bargained for. Josh had Marie Janeé pressed up against a wall. He was kissing her hot and heavy, and she was pushing back. I was about to step in when she kneed him in the groin and he doubled over. I ducked back around the corner and waited to see if she needed me. There may or may not have been a smile on my face.

"Jesus, Mary Jane." He was gasping so she must not have gotten him as hard as I wished. "Too good for me now, are you? Don't forget I made you. Right down to that phony name."

"I told you I'd get you the gig. I didn't agree to any side benefits. That was over a long time ago."

"Well, the gig is nice, but I expected a little more gratitude from you."

"Three thousand dollars for a one-hour show with a three-person cast? What are you paying them? Not much, I bet. So, you've got yourself a couple grand worth of gratitude."

"And the rock on your hand is worth ten times that."

Three thousand dollars? I don't mind Josh making a profit but sheesh. That was at least a thousand over what he usually charged. And we were getting the same pay rate.

Marie Janeé made a yelping sound and I peeked around the corner. He had her back up against the wall again. I marched in place a few steps, vigorously shaking my feet. The jingle bells did the trick. I walked around the corner as Josh jumped back.

"Hey. I'm sorry—where's the elevator?"

"I'm heading that way; I can show you." Marie Janeé strode down the hall, leaving Josh in her wake.

We walked back towards the lobby.

"Such an unpleasant little man," she said.

"I can't say I disagree. You might want to stop in and fix your lipstick." I pointed to a ladies' room up ahead.

"Thanks. Sorry I was a bitch earlier. I'm just…" she shrugged.

"It's okay. Just wish you'd kneed him harder."

She laughed. "Yeah. I have to learn not to pull my punches."

"Watch out for Edward, too."

"Don't I know it. There's a reason Irene drinks."

"No worries."

We split off and I followed the arrows to the lobby. Laura was there, in her party dress, looking distressed.

"They're starting to sit down for dinner. Have you seen Josh?"

The trick to lying well is to never hesitate, never elaborate. "Nope."

"If you see him, tell him to get in here." She headed past me, down the hallway towards the Green Room.

"Will do." I said over my shoulder and made a beeline for the elevator. No way was I going to get into the middle of this one. I hoped Josh would check himself for any tell-tale signs of his aborted make-out session. I was pretty sure he would; he never met a mirror he didn't love. I heard Laura say "There you are" as the elevator doors closed.

I went up to my room to change out of my costume and wash my face. The makeup made me itchy. I threw on jeans and a sweater and headed back to the elevator, happy not to be jingling for the first time in two hours.

Herbie, Dan, and Colin were already there when I arrived. Herbie was still dressed in his "backstage blacks" and Dan and Colin had changed back into street clothes. I noticed Dan hadn't quite gotten all his makeup off—I could still see the faint shadows of two round red circles on each of his cheeks. I wondered if my cheeks matched.

Staff dining was a buffet. You went down the line and got to choose what you wanted and as much as you wanted. The guys had full plates and I suspected they would go in for seconds. The food looked good. I might go in for seconds myself. I got a plate (rare roast beef with mashed potatoes, carrots, and a warm dinner roll with real butter). I didn't see where we could get an alcoholic beverage so I opted for a bottled water. It's nice to have a "wind-down" drink after a show, but not having one wouldn't kill me. I had better stuff upstairs.

"At least the food is good," Dan said, not quite having finished the food that was in his mouth.

"No complaints. But I thought there was a bar."

Colin shook his finger at Herbie. "Only ONE drink, Herbie."

"Jeez, could you believe that? As if we're children. Totally insulting." Herbie buttered his roll aggressively.

"He does like to throw his weight around," Dan said.

"Not to worry, the gift shop has alcohol, even if it's a bit overpriced."

The guys looked at me.

"Okay, a LOT overpriced. But bound to be cheaper than the bar."

"I'll grab some beer before I head back up," Dan said.

"And a midnight snack," Herbie put in.

Our conversation moved on to the show and the audience and our next show coming up. Truth be told, I worked with these guys a few times a month, but I didn't really know them well. Herbie pretty much kept to himself; he was a little on the outside as the tech guy. I knew Dan was taking acting classes and trying to break into the business. I had no idea about Colin. He was just... strange. Kind of nerdy but outgoing, too. The talk was superficial, at best. And that was fine with me. I was a bit tired—being outgoing and cheerful for an hour usually required a couple hours of recovery.

"I've been looking all over for you four," Josh bustled in.

"Aren't you supposed to be having dinner with the muck-ety-mucks?" Colin asked.

"No one's seen Marie Janeé. Have any of you seen her?"

The guys shook their heads.

He had missed a smudge of lipstick on his collar. The old song ran through my head.

"I saw her head into the ladies' room near the lobby before dinner. Did you see her after that?" I looked him straight in the eyes.

He broke eye contact, his face flushing a bit. "We're going to need you to check around the hotel, see if you can find her. We're having dinner, but Stephen is not happy and we need to find her."

"I don't see how this is our problem," Colin ventured.

"We're being helpful to the nice man who paid us and is putting us up at this nice hotel. Now get moving. I'll be in the dining room." He hurried out the door.

"Heaven forbid he should have *his* meal interrupted," Herbie said.

"I'm finishing what I have," I said. "She probably just went upstairs to reapply her makeup."

"It has been almost forty-five minutes," Colin said.

"Maybe she likes to make an entrance," I was focusing on the mashed potatoes, with the intent of not missing out on the chocolate cake I had chosen for dessert. "Five more minutes won't make a difference."

"I'm getting another dessert then," Dan said.

"Find out how late they're open. I might want coffee later."

Colin looked at me. "Coffee? At this hour?"

I put on a stoner voice. "Comics live on the edge, man." I finished my potatoes, shifted the dessert plate in front of me, and dug into the cake. It was pretty damn good.

Dan came back with some sort of apple crumble thing. My brain locked on: *That looks like it will go well with coffee later.*

"How do you want to do this?" I asked.

"What?"

"The search?"

"Well, I guess the first thing we do is check to see if she showed up at the dinner." Colin shrugged. "I'm not going to spend half an hour searching for someone who has already been found. I am off the clock."

"Smart," Dan said, swallowing a huge bite. "I guess we should check the event room, the Green Room, and the common areas after that."

"I'll take that," Herbie volunteered.

"It's not like we can go knocking on guest room doors," I said.

"I'll check the bar, gift shop, and salon area," Colin said.

"That leaves the pool and work out rooms for me," Dan wiped his mouth, the apple crumble a mere memory.

"I can check all the ladies' rooms and if there's a women's locker room or whatever."

"What about the grounds?"

"It's pouring buckets out there. I'm not going out."

"She wouldn't have gone out anyway. There would be no reason," I said.

They nodded.

We took our trays and plates over to the area set aside for that.

We went to the main dining room first and I peeked in. People were seated at round tables and there was a head table of sorts with what I assumed was the C-suite level people. A row of middle-aged and older white men with younger wives. The seat next to Stephen was empty.

"She's not there."

"Great," Herbie said.

"Let's just do this. Meet back at the Green Room?" Colin said.

"Works for me. Shouldn't take long."

We headed off in separate directions. None of us hurried. I guess we all figured she would turn up when she wanted to make her entrance.

I decided I would keep her little dalliance with Josh to myself, but I couldn't help but wonder if maybe she had a better offer somewhere else.

I checked my areas and met up with Dan at the pool. We walked back to the Green Room together. Colin was coming towards us from the other direction. We walked into the room and Colin flipped on the lights. Everything looked normal. Herbie came in through the event room door.

"Anything?"

"Nope."

"Looks normal here," I said. "Except... We packed the props, right? I didn't dream that?"

The props were in a pile next to the trunk. As if someone had scooped them out and dumped them.

Dan said. "Crap! Someone took all the props out again."

"There's nothing in there worth stealing," Colin said.

Herbie quickly checked the corner where his equipment was stored. "Nothing's touched here."

"Probably Josh, making sure he had something to yell at us about," Dan grumbled.

"Well, let's get it done and we can go drink. We're due." Colin walked over and lifted the lid. "Oh, sweet Jesus!" He almost fell backwards getting away from the trunk.

"What?" I looked in and recognized the blonde hair and dress. Marie Janeé. Now covered with blood. Our prop icicle was sticking straight out of her chest.

"Dan, run to the front desk and get security."

Dan's eyes were huge. "Is she... dead?"

Herbie took a look in the trunk and started gagging. I hoped he spotted the wastebasket.

"Go now!"

Dan hit the door like he was being chased by ghosts. I backed away from the trunk and looked at Colin.

"You okay?"

"No."

"Me, either."

"Herbie?"

"Oh, man. That's horrible. The poor woman."

At least he wasn't throwing up.

"What do we do?"

"Nothing. We wait."

"This is so not good."

We sat down. A couple of minutes later, Dan returned with a security guard. His reaction to the body in the trunk was on par with ours. When he recovered, he shifted into authoritarian mode.

"None of you move!"

"None of us has moved. We were waiting for you."

"Yeah, well, just don't go anywhere. I, uh, need to, uh…"

"Call the manager and get him or her here," I supplied. Probably a him, I thought.

He nodded and hit some numbers on a cell phone, then spoke briefly.

We all waited, looking at each other. The manager came flying through the door. A him. He looked in the trunk and gagged. To be fair, it was a lot of blood.

He looked around, not quite sure what to do. "Who found her?"

"We did. We were together and Colin opened up the trunk and…" I trailed off.

"Do you know who it is?"

"Marie Janeé Vashon. The people having the event here? The CEO's wife."

The manager went white. He pointed to the security guard. "Okay, right. Ray, you need to stay here. You four," he hesitated. "I don't know."

He pulled his cell phone out of his pocket and dialed 911.

"Deputy is on his way. Ray, secure the room and then we all need to wait outside. We're not supposed to touch anything."

"We need to tell her husband," I said.

"I don't think you four should leave the area."

"We're on an island and it's pouring outside. We're not going anywhere."

He nodded. "Follow me." We went back towards the lobby. He motioned us to a sitting area. "Wait here." Then he headed off down the hallway to the banquet room. I saw him square his shoulders before he went in. Poor guy.

Dan looked around at us. "Are we in some sort of trouble?"

"No, but it's going to be a long night." Not my first rodeo.

"What do you mean?"

"We're going to be questioned and then everyone is going to be questioned and pretty much it's going to be..."

"Bad," Colin said. "Long and bad."

"But we didn't do anything," Dan said.

I was thinking about the bottle of Macallan single malt in my room. "Nope. Doesn't matter."

The manager came back down the hallway with Stephen behind him, visibly upset. They rushed past us, heading for the Green Room. I looked out the lobby doors. In the distance I could see blue lights flashing. The cavalry was on its way.

Not a Good Shade for Him

WE WATCHED THE MANAGER greet the deputy and they walked back down towards the Green Room. We were admonished to stay where we were. The desk clerk kept looking over at us as if we were guilty of something, but she hadn't figured out what it was. Stephen hadn't come back down the hallway. I didn't know if he was in a private office or the event room. I sincerely hoped he wasn't in the Green Room with his wife's body.

Josh came down the hallway that led to the banquet room and stopped short when he saw us all sitting in the lobby.

"You were supposed to be finding Marie Janeé. Now Stephen has to go looking for her. And you definitely should *NOT* be sitting in the lobby. This area is for guests. You people are worse than useless. Did you even look?"

"We looked." Colin said flatly.

"We found her," I said.

"Good. Get up to your rooms then. You shouldn't be hanging around here."

We all looked at each other. Actually, Colin, Dan, and Herbie were looking at me.

"Marie Janeé is dead. We're waiting to talk to the police." I was purposely direct. I watched his reaction.

"That's not funny."

"Not being funny. We found her in the props trunk."

He looked at me, disbelieving and confused. "You must have made a mistake." He turned and walked down the hallway that led to the Green Room and event room. A minute later, he was back, looking grey. He took a seat next to Herbie.

"This is a disaster. I'll be ruined." Leave it to Josh to think of himself first.

"Yeah, Marie Janeé isn't doing so good either," Colin said. I gave him a tight smile.

"I should go tell Laura," Josh said. Apparently, he wasn't getting the sympathy he needed from us.

"I don't think you should go back into the banquet room and mention that the CEO's wife is dead," I said. "I'm sure people are already wondering what's going on and you popping in and whispering something shocking to Laura is not going to help." I tried to keep the irritation out of my voice, but really, the man had no sense of decency. "I'm pretty sure the deputy should be in charge of that."

I didn't envy the deputy. There must have been fifty people that he'd need to interview. Plus us. Plus hotel staff. I wondered when his back-up would arrive.

The hotel manager and the deputy came into the lobby.

"We're going to need you to come into the banquet room," the hotel manager said. He seemed used to organizing things. We stood up and followed him. I figured the deputy would have the unwanted task of announcing Marie Janeé's death.

People were lingering over coffee and dessert. There seemed to be a lot of after-dinner drinks on tables, too. When the boss is paying, everyone orders top shelf. One of the executives was giving a little end-of-year talk and he paused as we came into the room, then plowed on. We sat at an empty table in the back of the room. The deputy made his way to the head table and interrupted the speaker. He handed over the microphone to the deputy, looking more than a little put out to lose his moment in the spotlight. Whatever he had been saying would be forgotten in the next minute.

The deputy cleared his throat and winced a bit as the sound came over the speakers. "I'm Deputy Travis Fletcher with the Lee County Sheriff's Department. I have some um, sad news…" he cleared his throat again. "It's my duty to inform you that Marie Janeé Vashon has been found dead. And I…" he stopped as the room immediately filled up with exclamations and the buzzing of voices. He looked around helplessly and made several starts, trying to get people's attention.

I leaned over to Colin. "Something tells me our young deputy is out of his depth."

"Not a problem." Colin stood up, put his fingers in his mouth, and let out an incredibly loud whistle. "Oy!" he said in his elf character voice. "The deputy needs to speak."

The group immediately quieted down.

"A Christmas miracle."

"Five years as a camp counselor is more like it. These people are worse than kids."

I nodded and turned my attention to the deputy.

"I know this is a shock and I um…" He stopped and appeared to be doing a rough head count.

"It may just have dawned on him that he has a roomful of people to question," I whispered to Colin.

"Hope his back-up gets here soon. I just want to sit in that bathtub with a decent drink and watch TV."

I nodded. The exact thought had been playing in my mind since I first saw the bathroom set up.

The deputy squared his shoulders. "If someone could get me a list of guest names…"

The hotel manager waved his hand. "I'll have that for you in just a few minutes."

"Thank you. Um, obviously, I will need to talk to everyone here—"

"Are you saying we're suspects?" one of the execs at the head table asked.

"No. Well, yes, actually."

The room started buzzing again.

Colin let out a whistle and the noise died down immediately.

I looked over at him. "Impressive."

"I've also done some dog training."

Deputy Fletcher continued. "I uh, just need to know if anyone saw Mrs. Vashon between the show and dinner. If anyone did, I'd like to talk to you first so we can establish a timeline." He nodded to himself and repeated "timeline" under his breath. Unfortunately, the mic picked it up.

"This poor guy," I said.

Herbie nodded. "This is way above his pay grade."

Dan looked around. "Shouldn't there be more cops here for a murder?"

Colin pulled out his phone and did a quick search. "Nokosi Island has three full time deputies. They are under the jurisdiction of Lee County."

"So, they live here? They must get paid pretty well," Dan said.

"There's a question. Maybe they take the ferry over for their shifts. They live on the mainland." I thought about it. "In which case, it's going to take a while for his back up to arrive."

"Maybe longer than that," Colin held up his phone, showing a weather app. "Maritime warnings, low visibility, high winds."

"No one's coming until tomorrow at the earliest." Herbie's voice was flat.

"Fantastic." Dan slumped in his chair.

"You guys left the Green Room a little before I did. Did you see Marie Janeé?

They shook their heads.

That left me as one of the last people to see her alive. *Great.*

The deputy was conferring with the executive who had been speaking. Decisions were being made. Rather, the deputy was being managed. He spoke into the mic again.

"I'll need to speak with each of you at some point over the next twenty-four hours. I know it's late and this has been, uh, upsetting news. Since I have a list of all the attendees and obviously, no one is going anywhere, it may be best that we speak in the morning."

"What the hell?" I said.

"Sounds good to me," Dan said, standing up.

"Seriously?"

Herbie was beside him. "Like the man said, we're not going anywhere. If the cop wants us, he can find us. I'm going to see if I can get my equipment back."

The deputy continued talking, a bit of panic in his voice as people started gathering their things and pushing back their chairs.

"But if anyone saw Mrs. Vashon after the show and before dinner, I would like to talk to you tonight!"

I turned to Colin. "Oh man, he got totally managed. Normally, the police talk to everyone, at least for a few minutes, before letting them go. Get names, contact info..."

"Well, they've got that info from the hotel. And practically speaking, he's one guy. It would take all night."

I nodded and we stood up to leave. The deputy's voice came over the mic.

"You two. Actor people. I need to speak with you."

People looked at us on their way out. Josh and Laura took their time getting over to us, as if they didn't want to be associated with possible murderers. Really, Josh hardly wanted to be associated with us at all, so... nothing new there. Laura had Josh's suit jacket on over her shoulders. She looked paler than usual. Obviously, Josh had filled her in on the details.

"I'm going to head back to the room," she said. Between the boat ride over and this, I had a feeling her dinner wasn't going to stay down long.

The deputy made his way to our back table.

"Where are the other two?" he asked.

"They headed back to their rooms. They said if you need them, you can find them."

"I'll get with them. You two found the body?"

We nodded.

"What were you doing in that room?"

"Josh had sent us looking for Mrs. Vashon. She hadn't shown up at dinner."

"Why would he ask you to do that?"

"We serve at his pleasure," Colin said.

Josh jumped in. "Mr. Vashon asked me to check for her. He was at the head table, so he couldn't very well go looking. And it was embarrassing for her to be so late."

"Why did he ask you?" The deputy pursued it. I didn't know if he was stupid or very smart.

Josh flushed a bit. He started carefully. "Marie Janeé had been my point of contact for this event." He made a decision. "We've known each other for years and probably Mr. Vashon just turned to me because I wasn't involved in the dinner activities and no one would miss me."

A thought popped into my head. *It's more likely Mr. Vashon noticed his wife's lipstick on your collar and thought you'd know where to find her.*

"You knew Mrs. Vashon before this?"

I watched Josh's Adam's apple bob a couple of times in his throat. This would be enjoyable if the poor woman wasn't dead. Well, it was a little enjoyable watching Josh sweat anyway.

"Uh, yes. She had been an actress. Singer, dancer. She had worked in a few of my shows before meeting Mr. Vashon."

The deputy wrote this down. "And so, Mrs. Vashon hired your troupe to entertain at the party."

"Yes. Sir."

"And you decided to delegate the search."

"I figured four people looking would find her faster."

And you wanted to get back to the party with the muckety-mucks. Josh was excellent at delegating anything he didn't want to do.

"I'll need to speak to the other two after this."

"They didn't see anything until Colin opened the props trunk," I put in. "We put the props away, we all went up to our rooms, then went down to the staff dining room. Josh came in and asked us to look for Mrs. Vashon."

"And?"

"We split up. We searched and all met back in the Green Room."

"The *Green* Room?"

"Our backstage area," Josh supplied.

"Hey! That door should have been locked," Colin said. "All of Herbie's equipment is in there."

I looked at Josh. "Did you lock it?"

"Of course, I locked it."

I doubted it. Josh was fully flushed now. He was probably so pre-occupied with Marie Janeé's brush off and getting to dinner with the elite, that he didn't bother. Then I wondered if it was more than the encounter with Marie Janeé that had him nervous.

The deputy picked up on it, too. "Are you sure you locked it? This is important."

Josh cleared his throat. "I was running a little late so I figured I would go lock up after the dinner."

"Because who cares if Herbie's equipment is stolen, right?" Colin whispered to me. I nodded.

Josh was shooting me warning looks. I knew what he was worried about. I waited for the deputy to ask if any of us had seen Marie Janeé after the show, but he didn't. I figured once he got over being rattled and got his head in the game, that question would present itself. Josh was a lot of things, but I didn't think he had—frankly—the guts to kill someone. I wasn't ready to throw him under the bus yet. But we would be having a come-to-Jesus shortly. I gave him my best level gaze. The boys didn't know it, but we were getting a Christmas bonus.

"Isn't it usually the husband who does these things?" Colin asked.

Deputy Fletcher looked up, realizing he had left Mr. Vashon unattended. He covered quickly "Usually. But Mr. Vashon was with people the entire time, from before the show through the dinner."

He closed up his notebook. "I'll need to speak with all of you again."

We nodded and watched him silently as he walked away.

"Holy shit!" Josh said, his body sinking into the chair.

"Yeah, real cool, Josh. You didn't act nervous at all." I couldn't resist needling him.

"That's not funny," he snapped. "This reflects very badly on us." He was visibly upset. Can't say I blamed him considering what I had seen in the hall.

"How so? We just came in and did a show. Not our fault the wife got murdered," Colin shrugged. "It was probably the husband. He could have hired someone. He's rich enough."

"It will be big news for a couple of days in the business sections of the local papers and then no one will care," I said. The news moves on rapidly.

"I need a drink," Josh said.

"The gift shop has wine and beer," I said helpfully.

Josh nodded. I wondered if Laura had noticed the lipstick on Josh's collar. I was pretty sure she had. I figured they would have some talking to do

As if by mutual agreement, Colin and I sat and watched him go. It was more that we didn't want to get stuck hanging out with Josh than anything.

"I notice you didn't offer up any of your room booze to him," he said.

"Neither did you. Besides, my scotch is too good for him."

"So's my bourbon."

We had to pass the bar to get to the lobby elevators. Some of the event guests were in there, putting down more liquor. These people could drink. I had a sudden thought.

"We should have a drink here first."

"Why?"

"People talk when they're drunk. Maybe we'll learn something that poor deputy can use." Really, I'm just nosy.

Colin nodded. "Yeah, he could use some help."

We walked in and were immediately greeted by Edward and Irene.

"The elves! Hello elves!" Irene was effusive. I was afraid she was going to hug us.

"How did you recognize us without our clever disguises?" I asked.

They laughed too hard at the joke.

"What are you drinking?"

I went with a Cape Cod, which Edward upgraded to a top shelf vodka. I didn't want to tell him that I really couldn't taste the difference. Colin went with a Guinness.

"Terrible news about Mrs. Vashon," I said once the drinks were in front of us.

"Too bad, so sad," Irene sing-songed.

Edward was more circumspect. He shot her a sharp look. She rolled her eyes but managed to put on a serious face. "I am sure Stephen is devastated."

We nodded.

"I guess no one knows how she was killed," Edward ventured, clearly fishing.

"I think the deputy has to wait for the coroner or something," I said.

Colin was staring into his beer. "There was a lot of blood."

I took his hand under the table and squeezed it.

"Colin found her," I explained.

"Oh, my. Poor dear." Irene got all motherly but her eyes were gleaming. Could have been the alcohol, but I doubted it.

"Where did you find her?" Edward asked.

Colin was about to answer, but I interrupted him. "The deputy said we're not supposed to talk about the specifics of the um, case." I threw him a bone. "But it wasn't pretty. We're pretty shaken up."

Edward nodded sympathetically. "Of course."

Irene picked up the lead. "But it obviously happened between the show and dinner."

"Yes. At least the time of death is narrowed down." I looked at her. "Did you see her in the banquet room?"

They both thought back, then shook their heads.

Another couple joined us, the executive who had been giving the speech and his wife. Edward made the introductions.

"Trip, Judy, this is... Sorry. I don't know your real names." He gave a small, embarrassed laugh.

"Kasey McCormick."

"Colin Stone."

We didn't shake hands.

"Colin found Marie Janeé," Irene said.

They both looked at us again. We were now worthy of interest.

Trip said, "A terrible thing." Judy made a little murmuring noise.

"Edward and Irene said that they didn't see Marie Janeé in the banquet room. Did you?"

They shook their heads.

"She would have been hard to miss, too. All that red."

"Not to mention the rock on her hand," Irene snarked.

Judy bugged her eyes out a bit in agreement. They weren't wrong. Marie Janeé had had a honking diamond on her hand. I pictured her in my mind. She had been wearing a diamond tennis bracelet as an anklet, a couple of expensive bangle bracelets as well as a pricey necklace.

I forced myself to remember what she looked like in the props trunk. Did I see any jewelry? I thought she still had it on, but I couldn't be sure. A shiver ran through my body.

"Poor dear," Irene said. "Do you need another drink?"

"Better not. I'm not sure if we're even allowed in here." I stage whispered, "We're the help."

They laughed as if we were all equals. But we weren't. I nudged Colin with my knee.

Colin picked right up on my nudge. One of the many reasons I liked working with him. He finished his Guinness. "We better be getting back to our rooms before the boss catches us."

We said our thanks and goodnights and I glanced back at the four-some left at the table. The men's heads were together, already deep in discussion. I didn't know if they were talking about Marie Janeé or plotting to take over the company. Either way, they weren't letting the grass grow under their feet.

Tenser is the Night

THE RED LIGHT WAS blinking on my room phone when I got in. I hit the code for voice mail. "Kasey, we need to talk. Tonight." Josh's voice was just above a whisper. I figured he called as soon as Laura was in the bathroom. Didn't want to text me, either. I wondered if Laura checked his phone. She didn't seem the type, but then again, he was the type to check his significant other's phone. Guys like Josh assumed everyone was as devious as they were.

I don't know how I was supposed to get in touch with him. I didn't care. I had the upper hand for a change and I was happy to let him sweat.

I had left the TV on, a habit I picked up to make people think there was someone in the room. Thieves look for empty rooms; they don't want to run the risk of being caught. They hear a TV, they move on to the next room. At least, that's the theory. I flipped through channels, and came across the beginning of *Love Actually*. I probably have watched it over a dozen times and I will most likely watch it multiple times a year until I die. I got my PJs out of the drawer and was about to pull my sweater over my head when there was a light knock on the door.

Crap.

I looked through the peephole. Josh. Of course. I let him in.

He didn't waste time on pleasantries. "I don't know what you think you saw tonight, but it wasn't anything. I've known Marie Janeé for years. That was just a little old times' sake fooling around."

"None of my business, Josh. Though I don't think she wanted to reminisce with you."

"What did she say?"

"That she needs to learn not to pull her punches. Or kicks."

"Not funny."

"We walked down the hall together and she hit the ladies' room to fix her lipstick." I touched his collar. "Something you need to take care of, too."

He looked in the mirror. "Crap. Do you think Laura saw this?"

She hadn't mentioned it yet. "You should be more worried about whether or not the deputy saw it. Or Stephen Vashon."

His eyes widened. He sat down on the bed hard.

Great. Now I'll never get rid of him. I checked the TV. Colin Firth was getting ready to go to the wedding, unaware that his girlfriend was trying to get him out of the house. I knew how she felt.

"I had nothing to do with her death."

"I didn't think you did."

"Laura agreed that this is going to be bad press for us."

No surprise there. Laura agreed with just about everything Josh said. "There will most likely be *no* press for us. We are minor players here, Josh. Not the headliner."

He took this in, then gathered himself up.

"Still, it would be better if we kept this between us."

"I'm not going to lie to the police for you, if that's what you're saying. If the deputy asks, I'll let him know. And you should, too. Maybe you should volunteer that information. It would look better for you."

He nodded and started for the door.

"One other thing."

He turned.

"You got at least an extra thousand dollars for this show. I am sure you were going to give us all a surprise bonus, yes?"

"Are you blackmailing me?"

"No. I already told you I wasn't going to lie to the deputy. This is separate. I'm talking about a little Christmas spirit here. Or maybe hazard pay, if you like."

"I'll think about it."

To his credit, he didn't slam the door.

I unmuted the TV and got into my flannel Red Sox jammies. I took out my bag of Twizzlers and poured myself a healthy glass of Macallan twelve. Settling in on my bed, I was determined to forget the events of the night. The pop-up wedding chorus was singing *Love, Love, Love.* I love, love, loved this scene.

Another knock on my door.

"For the love of all that is holy!" I muted the TV and went to the door. I looked through the peephole again. Colin, Herbie, and Dan. I sighed, then opened the door, mentally giving up on the movie.

"Can we come in?" Dan asked.

Colin held up a six pack. His bourbon must have been too good for Dan and Herbie, too. "We come bearing gifts."

"Are you guys kidding me?" I let them in.

"I guess you were getting ready for bed," Dan said.

I looked down at my pajamas. "What gave it away?"

"We thought you might be scared."

I gave them a look.

"Well, okay. We're all a little freaked out and we figured you would be, too."

"I am, a bit." I looked around and sighed. "Make yourselves comfortable.

Colin looked at the bottle on the bedside table. "Nice. I guess you don't need my beer."

"Thanks all the same."

"Scotch? I can't drink that stuff," Herbie said.

"It's an acquired taste."

"I can't believe you thought to bring booze with you," Dan said.

"I don't usually, but Josh was so pissy about us having one drink…"

"I bet he's having more than one right now," Herbie said.

"He and Laura think this will bring us bad press," I said.

"Do you think so?"

I shook my head. "Not really. I doubt if we get any press. But he has mentioned it twice. That means he's already trying to figure out a PR angle on this."

"Tacky," Colin said. I nodded.

Colin and Herbie sat in the chairs at the little table set-up. Dan looked around, helped himself to a beer and then stretched out on the other bed. He looked up at the TV. "I love this movie." He reached for the remote to unmute it. I snatched it back.

"My room. My remote." I don't share well with others in the best of times. I looked at them. They were looking at me expectantly. "Are we going to all share our feelings?"

"I'm pissed that Josh didn't lock up the Green Room. I could have lost all my equipment!" Herbie said.

"I don't think she meant those kinds of feelings," Colin pointed out.

"But your feelings are valid, Herbie." I smoothed things over. "What are you guys thinking?"

They looked at Colin. He started. "First, I don't think we're getting off this island tomorrow." He held up his phone to show the weather app. "They've suspended the ferry runs because of the storm. Maybe we'll get out late in the day, but it's doubtful."

I nodded. And started thinking about calling in late to work on Monday. At least I had extra clothes with me. I could go straight there.

"So, we're stuck in a fancy hotel for an extra day. I'm pretty sure they'll comp our meals and room if the cops are forcing us to stay. Or the company will pay for them."

"You're not getting it." Dan bobbed his head, nudging.

"What?"

"We're stuck on an island in a storm with a murderer. Duh."

I laughed. "Ooooh. Scary."

They didn't say anything.

"C'mon guys. This has nothing to do with us." I looked at Colin. "You said it was probably the husband. It usually is in these cases."

"Yeah, but what if it's not? She and Josh worked together doing shows. What if it's tied into that?"

"Then Josh should worry. Not us. We never met any of these people before tonight."

"So, you're saying we just wait it out and leave when the ferry starts running."

"Unless one of you killed her." I looked at them. No takers. "I've made my point. Now can I go back to my movie?"

"Cool." Dan reached for the remote and turned the sound back on. He settled back on the bed. "Do you guys want some pizza or something from room service?"

"We just ate!" I was picturing pizza grease all over the room.

"That was almost two hours ago," Dan said. He had a point.

"Where's the menu?" Colin was sorting through the hotel literature on the table.

Herbie cracked open another beer. "We might need more beer."

I closed my eyes and took a deep breath. Then I settled back onto my bed. Might not be the worst thing to have company tonight.

Do Not Threaten Me Before I've Had My Coffee

I HAD PLANNED TO sleep in. My cell phone had different ideas. The room clock read 8:15. Ugh. I looked at the caller ID. Josh. Double Ugh.

"Yes. What?" I wasn't even pretending to be pleasant.

"We're meeting the deputy in the event room. He wants to talk to all of us."

"When?"

"As soon as possible."

"My soon as possible will not be super-soon. Are you rolling the guys out of bed?"

"Laura is calling them. I just want you to remember what we discussed last night."

"Yes. And you need to remember what I told you." I clicked off. *Don't wake me up and try to threaten me. I need coffee first.*

I could hear rain beating against the window. No surprise there; the wind had been howling all night. I parted the curtain and saw nothing but wet greyness. We weren't going anywhere soon. The room had a slight, lingering odor of eau de frat party. We had a neatly assembled collection of beer bottles by the wastebasket. Herbie had made a quick beer run down to the gift shop. I had stuck with my scotch. We'd had a good time. *Love Actually* ended and then a mindless and predictable Christmas romance started, and we all started making fun of it, making up lines for the actors. It was the wee small hours of the morning by the time the guys left. If you were going to be stuck on an island, they were a fun group to get stuck with.

Thirty minutes later I was showered and dressed, with just enough makeup applied to not scare people. If you didn't look too closely at my eyes. I went down into the lobby and helped myself to the coffee that was set up there. No way was I walking into a meeting with the police without coffee. I could smell bacon all the way from the guest dining room. I wondered if we could eat there or if we'd be relegated to the staff dining room. From last night's dinner, I guessed staff dining would still be pretty good.

I was the last one to the meeting. The event room now had a table set up with a couple of chairs on either side. The extra tables and chairs were stacked against one wall. The guys had pulled down some chairs to sit on and Dan grabbed one down for me.

"Kasey, glad you could join us." Snark didn't look good on Josh. It just makes him look as petty as he actually is.

"If you wanted me here earlier, you should have called earlier." I am getting so much better at setting boundaries.

"We just got here, too," Dan said. He was oblivious to the darts Josh shot at him. "Can I go get coffee?"

"The deputy is going to be here any minute, so no," Josh said.

Colin looked at my coffee. "But he's not here now. We'll be right back."

"Bring some back for me." Josh said.

I heard one of the guys mumble, "Get it yourself."

"Laura, get us some coffee, will you, sweetie?"

She got up from her chair. "Sure, *sweetie*." Trouble in paradise. She had noticed the lipstick.

I hid my smirk behind the coffee cup. *Would Laura lie for him? Probably. But now he had two of us to worry about.*

"There's no need to tell the deputy about Marie Janeé and me."

"As I told you last night, if he asks me directly, I'm not going to lie."

"I'm not asking you to *lie*, just don't bring it up. There's such a thing as loyalty, you know."

"Yes, and it's usually earned."

"Well, that goes both ways. You can get a lot of work from me. Or… maybe you won't be able to find work at all."

"So, I'll never work in this town again? Ooooh. BFD, Josh. You produce dinner theatre. I think I'll be okay." My head was starting to hurt. One cup of coffee was not going to get me through this.

Deputy Fletcher walked through the door, carrying a cup of coffee. He held the door for Laura, who had coffee cups in both hands. The guys were right behind them. I took a good look at Fletcher. He was tall and well-built. Today he didn't look quite as lost as he had been last night. From the wrinkles in his clothes and the bags under his eyes, I surmised he had been up all night, probably on the phone with his supervisor. His eyes were red. He was running on no sleep and had a long day ahead of him. Poor guy.

He set his coffee cup on the table and leaned against it. "Thanks for coming. I need to go over the events of last night with each one of you, individually. I'll try to make it as quick as possible so you can get on with your day."

He had a slight southern accent, a bit more refined than I expected from a deputy sheriff in Lee County, Florida. That's what I get for stereotyping, even if it's just in my head. He looked at us and asked, "Who wants to go first?"

That surprised me. Normally, the cops take control over every little detail to establish their authority. Either he didn't know to do that or he was too tired to play games.

Dan volunteered to go first.

"If the rest of you could wait outside the room, there are some chairs set up in the hall."

Josh took a step forward. "I'd like to be in the room if you're questioning my people."

Fletcher looked at him for a few seconds. "Are you an attorney?"

"Um, no."

"Then no. I'm just establishing a time line here. You're not suspects. You can wait in the hall with the others."

Even Laura smirked at this comment. We obediently went out the door to wait. Five minutes later, Dan came out and said, "Next."

We all looked at each other. Herbie stood up. "Was it bad?"

"No. He just wanted to know what we were doing. Easy peasy."

Herbie went in. I went down the hall for more coffee. Dan was still there when I got back.

"Sticking around to give us moral support?" I asked.

"I figured we could all go into breakfast after this."

I could tell he still wasn't comfortable with the swankiness of the hotel. It was kind of cute. "Sounds good."

"Laura and I will be in the guest dining room."

"Yay for you?" Dan said. Colin snorted a bit of his coffee. Josh looked uneasy. Dissension in the ranks.

Herbie came out, looking relieved. He shook his head. "Easy."

Without any discussion about who was next, Colin went in. This was going fast and I could almost taste breakfast. I sat back in my chair to wait my turn. Laura and Josh could go last. There was food on my horizon.

Ten minutes in, I shifted in my seat. Apparently, Colin's interview was not as easy-peasy as the first two. I looked at Herbie and Dan and raised my eyebrows. They made eyes back at me. Josh and Laura were a little ways away from us. He was pretending to be busy with Laura, giving her instructions as if he were a big Broadway producer. We were all fine with that. Josh was the guy who paid us. We tried to have as little interaction with him as we could. Since he was also the director, talent coordinator, and booker, as well as producer, that was hard to do. We all learned our lines as quickly as possible, got the blocking laid out, hit our marks, and made sure we had no more rehearsals with him than were necessary. The shows themselves required less than an hour or so of dealing with him. I thought about how quickly the hours went by with the guys last night. Josh had a way of making time stand still. And it wasn't a good way.

Poor Laura. I looked over and saw her nodding at Josh's instructions, dutifully writing everything down. She was nice enough, but definitely on Team Josh. Well, as his girlfriend, she had to be. She looked like she was about to cry. I wasn't sure if it was because of the murder or because she had figured out Josh was cheating on her. Or at least tried to.

Josh was putting on a show—there was no reason for her to be taking notes. I don't know why he was trying to impress us. Maybe he was trying to re-establish himself as the man in charge after the deputy's snarky put down. If possible, Laura looked even more pale than last night. She had probably been thinking this gig would double as a romantic getaway with Josh. Not so much.

I didn't understand her attraction to Josh, but then again, sometimes people with unassuming personalities are happy to be part of the circle of people with large personalities. Josh certainly had that. I wondered if her attraction to him was strong enough to prevail against the no-way-to-hide-it lipstick evidence of his disloyalty.

Colin finally came out and nodded to me. He took the chair I was vacating.

"That took longer than the others," I pointed out.

"Don't I know it," he sighed.

"Why don't you guys go ahead to the staff dining room and I'll meet you there. If this takes too long, I don't want you keeling over from hunger."

They shuffled off as I went in and took a seat in front of Deputy Fletcher. He looked at his list.

"Kasey McCormick."

"That's me." In my head, I heard my mother say, *That's I. Predicate nominative.* I didn't correct myself. *Sorry, Mom.*

"You saw Mrs. Vashon in between the show and dinner, is that correct?"

"Yes." *Was it time to throw Josh under the bus already?*

"Tell me about that. Starting with leaving the, um, Meet and Greet." He seemed unfamiliar with the term. I had been, too, until I started doing shows with Josh.

"We left the Meet and Greet..."

"Who is we?"

"Oh. Colin, Dan, and I. Herbie had to stay in the event room until everyone left. Laura was already in the Green Room, I think." I wasn't sure and I was trying to remember back. "Laura had changed into her party dress. She asked us to pack up the props trunk so she could get to the Meet and Greet."

"All three of you packed the trunk."

"Yeah. There's not that much to it, but it has to go in a certain order. Cue cards get put in a plastic wrapper and go flat on the bottom. Lighter stuff goes on the top, the rubber chicken can go anywhere, the icicle..." I paused and shivered remembering the icicle sticking straight up out of Marie Janeé's chest. I realized I had been skipping over that picture in my mind.

"Were any of the props missing?"

"When we put them back in?" He nodded. "No. We have a check-list." I looked at the papers in front of him. "I see you do, too."

He moved the papers around, covering a few up.

"Who put the icicle in the trunk?"

"I don't know. It's one of the last things to go in because it's light. One of the guys."

He nodded and made a note. "So, it wouldn't have your finger-prints on it."

"I'm sure it does. It probably has all of our fingerprints on it. Laura usually lays out the props, but we pass props to each other, we help pack up."

"Does the sound guy—" he looked at his list. "Herbie handle the props?"

"Sometimes. He was still in the event room when we were packing up. I don't know if he touched the icicle last night or not."

"Do the props get wiped down after a show?"

I laughed. "Please. We're lucky if Dan washes out his tights after a show."

I got a little smile out of him.

"So, after you were done with the props trunk, you closed it."

"Dan did. Yeah."

"Does it get locked up?"

"No. Nothing in there is super valuable. The cape gets hung up. The top hat and the homburg have their own special boxes."

"Homburg?"

"It's a hat. Like a fedora." I figured he wouldn't care about the bah homburg joke.

"You all left the Green Room together."

"The guys left together. Laura and Herbie were in the event room at the Meet and Greet. I picked up my show things—brush, emergency lipstick, breath mints, sewing kit, that sort of stuff—and left. I was maybe a minute behind them."

"And then?"

"I thought I was heading for the elevators but I turned the wrong way and ended up by the pool." I paused. Time to spill the beans. "I saw Josh and Marie Janeé kissing. Actually, Josh was kissing her. She was pushing him away."

Now I had his interest. He straightened up. "You saw Josh and Marie Janeé together *after* the Meet and Greet."

"Don't get too excited. I went back around the corner and jingled my shoes..."

"You did what?"

"Oh, we wear these elf shoes and hats with jingle bells. I wasn't wearing the hat, but I still had the shoes on. If you walk softly, they don't make much noise. But if you shake or stomp your feet..." I let him draw the obvious conclusion.

"So, you had been walking *softly* down the corridor?"

"Deputy Fletcher, it's bad enough walking around dressed like an elf. You don't really want to call attention to yourself. Especially in a nice hotel." I took a breath. "Besides, we'd been jingling for an hour. It gets on your nerves."

"A little too merry?" He looked back at his notes. "You went back around the corner and uh, jingled." I nodded.

"Well, I was just going to walk back to the elevators, but then I wanted to make sure Mrs. Vashon was okay."

"Did you know Mrs. Vashon before?"

"No. But Girl Code. If you think there's a situation, you don't walk away."

He repeated "Girl code" under his breath.

"I listened to a bit of conversation and since Josh was being insistent, I jingled then came around the corner like I had just arrived."

"A little duplicitous, wasn't it?"

I shrugged, but mentally gave him points for using an SAT word.

"What happened next?"

Marie Janeé walked away from Josh and we headed back down the hallway together. She stopped off in the ladies' room to fix her makeup."

He shuffled some papers and brought out a hotel floor plan. "This ladies' room? Near the lobby?"

"Yeah."

"Did you see her after that?"

"No."

"What about Josh? He should have been not too far behind."

"He probably gave us a head start. Since his advances hadn't been successful, he probably wanted to give us a wide berth. Or he was having a little trouble walking." I didn't bother to hide my smile.

"The Green Room is between the lobby and that ladies' rest room. Did you see anyone else in the area?"

"Laura was in the lobby, looking for Josh. I told her I hadn't seen him." I was picturing it in my mind but something wasn't right. Deputy Fletcher didn't give me time to think.

"You lied?"

"Flat out."

"Because..."

"Laura is dating Josh. He's the guy who pays me. I was not going to get in the middle of that one."

He thought for a minute. He was framing a question and then decided against it.

"After you saw Laura?" It wasn't a full question, but I followed where he was going.

"I went up to my room, washed off the makeup, changed my clothes, and met up with the guys in the staff dining room."

"And that took how long?"

"I don't know, maybe fifteen minutes."

"At that point, you were with the three men until Josh came and asked you to search for Mrs. Vashon."

"Yes. We split up to search the different areas. We had agreed to meet back at the Green Room, mostly because we had to search the event room and the Green Room, too. Might as well all meet up there."

"That's when you found the body."

"We noticed that the props were dumped on the floor. We went to repack them and when Colin opened up the trunk..." I stopped, seeing it again in my mind. Colin screaming and jumping back. The rest of us checking the trunk to see inside. The blonde hair, red dress, and the icicle sticking straight up in her chest. "There was so much blood," I whispered.

"Do you need a minute?"

"I might need a lifetime to get over that."

"After that, what happened?"

"I sent someone—Dan, I guess, he's got the longest legs—to get security. The security guy came, freaked out. Called the manager. The manager freaked out and I guess they called you."

"Where were Josh and Laura all this time?"

"They were having dinner with all the corporate bigwigs."

"You saw them in there."

I thought back to when we checked the dining room to see if Marie Janeé had turned up. Josh and Laura had been sitting at one of the tables, glasses of wine in front of them. I nodded yes.

"Let's go back." I groaned inwardly. "Josh and Marie Janeé were having a fight. Was it just that he was coming on to her?"

"Sort of. He seemed to feel entitled to a little extracurricular activity and Marie Janeé was having none of it. He said that he had 'made her' and..." I stopped.

"What?"

"He said that he had made her, right down to her phony name. Her name is really Mary Jane. Anyway, she said that he was getting a higher rate for the show than normal and that should be good enough and that's about the time I started jingling."

"Did Josh seem threatening?"

"Josh is always threatening. It's his default. He's like a freakin' chihuahua."

This got an actual laugh out of Fletcher. I was insecure enough to count that as a major score.

"So, he was threatening her."

"Sort of but really, it was the normal Josh-level bullshit. He threatens, but he has no real juice. Typical bully. All wind, no punch."

"Anything else you'd like to add?"

"Just that when you present Josh with this information, you should know that he'll make my life miserable."

"Sorry about that. Will you get fired?"

"No." I grinned at him. "I wrote the show."

He nodded appreciatively. "I'll tell him I forced it out of you."

"Thanks. Is that all?"

"For now. Send in Laura. I'll save Josh for last."

"He's really harmless. I don't think he could do something like that."

"No one thinks someone is capable of it until they see it for themselves."

"No, I mean, he's a total wuss—squeamish. Doesn't like anything messy. Plus, he's lazy. You're the detective, but I don't think he's your guy."

"I'm just a deputy. I'm only in charge until the brainiacs get here."

I stood up to go, then stopped. "One other reason, then."

Fletcher looked at me.

"There was a lot of blood in that trunk. Josh didn't have anything red on him outside of Marie Janeé's lipstick. No one is that neat."

Deputy Fletcher leaned back in his chair, closed his eyes, and groaned. "I'm an idiot."

"You're one guy with a murderer, at least sixty suspects, and no back up."

He ever so slightly shook his head. "Even so."

"I'll send Laura in."

Bus Meet Josh

Both Laura and Josh looked up as I came through the door. I looked at Laura. "Your turn." I kept walking so that Josh didn't have time to ask me any questions. *Let him sweat.*

The guys were more than halfway through their food when I got there. I went down the buffet line, and got a plate loaded with freshly scrambled eggs, crisp bacon, and pancakes. I grabbed a little silver container of syrup and a bottled water. Then I hit the coffee station and filled a cup.

I set my plates of food on the table, along with my coffee and water and the syrup. Then I set the tray aside. The guys still had everything on their trays.

"How'd ya do?" Herbie asked.

"He asked, I answered."

Dan looked around and then leaned in conspiratorially. "Yeah, but who do you think did it?"

"Nobody we know. Or at least have known for more than a day." I ate a forkful of egg then spread some butter on my pancakes before they got cold. I doused them with syrup. Not real maple. I bet the guests got real maple.

The guys seemed to have recovered from the horror of last night. Maybe the few hours of watching mindless movies helped them distance themselves from it. The mind is very good at blocking out things it doesn't want to think about.

"I think the deputy thinks it was one of us," Colin looked at each of us.

"I think a few people in this room think so too, and the rest want to pump us for details. Look around."

"They're probably looking at Dan because he's so damn handsome," Colin kidded.

"'Tis true," Dan said. "That or because I'm freakishly tall." He made a face.

"Maybe they're just watching us because we don't really work here. We don't fit in." Herbie drank some orange juice but he looked around the room as if he were afraid the employees were going to close in with torches and pitchforks.

"Yeah, that's it. They're probably going to tell us where the smoking area is and which supervisor is handsy." I lowered my voice. "We should probably not talk about it when little ears are nearby."

"It's not like we're involved," Dan said.

"Dan, we found the body," Colin reminded him.

"Well, yeah. There's that."

We were all silent for a few seconds, remembering. I shifted the conversation to getting off the island. The storm seemed to be getting stronger and the fog did not look like it was going to lift any time soon.

I looked at Colin. "Have you checked the forecast?"

"Bad news on that."

"It's not letting up?"

"I don't know. Cable and internet are out."

"I wonder if the phone lines are down, too."

"Great. Just great." Dan said.

"You had a hot date?" Colin teased.

"Playoff game today?" He stuck out his chin to emphasize his point.

"Everyone's stuck here," I said. "Us. Guests, Employees."

"The murderer," Herbie said.

"It's like one of those movies." Dan started getting enthusiastic. "Everyone is weekending at a country house and there's a storm and the lights go out—"

"You better hope the lights don't go out. That means they can't cook the food." I have my priorities.

"Maybe they use gas," Herbie offered helpfully.

"Anyway, the lights go out and someone gets murdered, and they have to figure out who the murderer is... We should talk to Josh about adding a murder mystery show."

It wasn't a bad idea. The timing, however, was more than a bit cringe. I made a face at Colin.

"Maybe we should hold off on that idea for just a bit, Dan. You know, until we're off the island that we're stuck on..." Colin looked directly at Dan to see if he was getting it. "You know. With. The. Murderer."

Dan's eyes widened. The hypothetical hit reality. He leaned in.

"Do you think we're in danger?"

"Only if we keep blabbing about what we know in public." I didn't bother to keep the exasperation out of my voice. "Anybody asks, we found the body. It was horrible. We have no idea who did it. Not our circus."

"Not our monkeys," the three chorused. Thankfully it was sotto voce.

"Let's meet back in Kasey's room to talk about it," Colin said.

"Why my room?"

Colin shrugged. "Why not?"

"Not until I have more coffee. And maybe one of those cinnamon buns. They look made from scratch."

"I'm totally going back for that," Herbie was halfway out of his chair.

"Speaking of," I started. He sat back down. "Not that we should buy out the gift shop—"

"Not that we can afford to," Colin said.

"Truth. But if the electric goes out and we're all stuck here, you might want to load up on some snacky-snacks. And not just junk food and beer."

"Got it. No junk food or beer," Dan said.

"No, get the junk food and beer. But also get something that will be filling and at least slightly nutritious. Don't go crazy or anything, but you might want something in reserve."

"Good thinking," Herbie agreed.

"Do you think these people will go all *Lord of the Flies* if the electricity goes out?" Colin asked, giving me a skeptical look.

"One, points for citing *Lord of the Flies*."

"Thank you."

"Two, these people are very entitled and we're the help. It's going to dawn on them that they're stuck on an island with a murderer. They're already hiding the good jewelry."

Colin nodded. "You're right. We need to discuss this privately. We're low down on the food chain."

Dan glanced around the room. "What's our plan?"

I leaned in. They all leaned in with me. "First thing we do," I paused. "Is get more coffee and a cinnamon bun. And try to act natural." I grinned and got the laugh. "It's probably going to be fine. We won't lose power. The storm will pass. The ferry will come. And it will turn out the husband did it, just as Colin said."

The cinnamon buns were nothing short of amazing. Between the sugar rush and the coffee kicking in, I was ready to face the day. There would still be things to discuss, of course. I should probably tell them about Marie Janeé and Josh. We agreed to meet in my room in half an hour. We were clearing our plates when Josh walked in.

"We need to have a team meeting," he announced.

We sat back down.

"Not here. I've arranged for the conference room. Follow me." He turned on his heel. We all looked at each other and sighed.

"The king has summoned us," Colin whispered.

"And as we are sworn unto him, follow we must." Dan made a sweeping gesture with his arm and we all got moving. We followed Josh down a hallway, through the lobby and off to another hallway. The conference room was next to the business center. Laura was already seated. We sat down at one end of the conference table.

"This is looking very bad for us," Josh began.

My head hurt and I wasn't up for the gloom and doom lecture he was about to deliver.

"In what way, Josh? Because the way I see it, the only way we're involved is someone used our props trunk to hide the body. After we had all cleared out. So, maybe *you* have some stronger connection to this, but we don't." Bus meet Josh.

Josh flushed. His coloring did him no favors.

"Well, I did know Marie Janeé before this gig, of course," he started. I could see him getting defensive, ready to pull out some alternate version of the truth. Most people suck at lying. Me included. "But, of course, I had nothing to do with her death."

"No one thinks you did," Colin said. He looked around the table. "Anyone?"

Herbie shook his head no. Dan gave a short laugh.

"This isn't funny." Laura was defending her man. I guessed she had gotten past the lipstick.

"No, it's not. But, as I said, this isn't about us. We've given our statements; let the good deputy do his job. I'd rather know if the ferry is going to run today."

Josh shifted uncomfortably. "I talked with the hotel manager and he said ferry service is cancelled until tomorrow morning."

"So, we're stuck here," Dan said.

"Yes. But I've arranged a lower room rate for you—"

"WHAT?"

"Well, it's a hotel and the company only paid for one night of accommodations." Josh's voice had a whine in it.

"I'm not paying for my room," Colin stated flatly.

"I *can't* pay for my room," Dan admitted. "Even at a lower rate, this place is ridiculously expensive."

"It's not for us to pay, anyway," I said, looking straight at Josh. "Either you pay for the rooms or you get the client to pay. It's not on us." I pushed it just a bit. "I'm *very* sure this show made a profit. Our rooms can come out of that if the client won't pay."

Josh could see his tidy profit disappearing before his eyes.

Herbie sat back and folded his arms. We all looked at Josh. He had an insurrection on his hands.

"Well, yeah, most likely the client will pay, but Mr. Vashon as you would imagine, is not in a good place right now..."

"There's a second-in-command guy. Trip something. Find him. And don't ask. Just state it like it's a done deal." I thought for a second. "Make it matter of fact. Not a threat or a whine, Josh."

"I know how to talk to clients, Kasey."

I managed to not roll my eyes. Colin did, which made me smile. Josh, fortunately, didn't catch it.

"So, we're here until tomorrow morning," Laura tried to bring the meeting back under control. "You can continue eating in the staff dining room. The manager has comped your meals there."

"He hasn't seen how much Dan can eat," Herbie joked.

"Or Kasey." Dan passed the buck.

I didn't disagree. I can put away some food. It's one of my strengths.

"What are we supposed to do in the meantime?" Colin asked. I looked at him. We both knew what was coming.

"We're not guests of the hotel, so it is best that you keep to your rooms as much as possible. No using the pool or the weight room..."

"Oh man. That's not fair," Dan protested.

"Look, it's a bad situation and we need to make the best of it," Laura said.

"And will you two be stuck in your room?" Colin asked.

"Well, no. We need to coordinate with the client and the hotel manager, as well as the police..."

"Bullshit," Dan said. He slumped down in his chair.

"We're not children. We're not second-class citizens. We're adults who know how to behave in a nice hotel," Colin began. "We might not have full guest privileges, but if we want to take a walk, go to the gift shop, or even get a drink in the bar, we'll do that. But we're not going to stay cooped up in our rooms all day." He stood up.

"This meeting is not over," Josh said.

I stood up. Dan and Herbie followed.

"I think it is." Colin headed for the door and we followed, leaving Josh sputtering.

We made it to the hallway before we started giggling.

"This meeting is *NOT* over," Dan mimicked Josh.

"I think it is." Herbie played Colin. "That was awesome." Herbie patted Colin on the back.

We walked back to the lobby.

"Gift shop?" Dan asked.

"I'm going to take stock of what I have in my room," I said.

"I've got nuthin," Herbie commented.

"Okay. We've got all day and no Internet. Kasey, we'll meet back in your room in what, half an hour?" Colin looked at his watch.

"And do what?" I asked.

They looked at me in disbelief.

Dan broke the silence. "Solve the murder, of course."

Oy.

Where's Sean Bean When You Need Him?

Roughly half an hour later, there was a knock on my door. I took a look around the room. The maid had already been through and everything was neat and tidy. *Enjoy it now. The guys will have it torn apart in two minutes.* I sighed and opened the door.

They bundled in, full of enthusiasm. Colin handed me a cup of coffee and pulled a couple of sugar packets out of his jeans pocket. "I already added cream."

"Thanks." He might look like a wild man, but he had obviously been brought up right. I mentally dropped him in my "civilized" box. It was a game I played in my head, a different version of "Dead, Alive, or Canadian." I mentally categorized men as Feral, Civilized, and Predators. Not politically correct, I know, but alarmingly useful. Herbie and Dan were still young enough to be classified as Feral. Eventually, they'd gain some polish and end up in the Civilized category. Josh was firmly in the Predator category. But he was a money predator, not a horn dog. For the most part.

Dan took the other bed again, his long legs stretched out with just his feet hanging off the edge. I sat cross-legged on my bed, mostly so none of the guys would think it was open territory. Colin had already put his coffee on the table.

I looked at Dan. "Your meeting."

He sat up smoothly, swinging his long legs back down to the floor. His face was alive with enthusiasm.

"I've been thinking about this…"

"That's dangerous," Colin threw out the obvious line.

Dan grinned and went on. "So, if we can solve this murder, we can use it to create our own murder mystery show. I can play the detective. There'd be parts for all of us. Kasey all you need to do is write it up!"

I closed my eyes for a few seconds. I decided to ignore his assumption that writing an interactive show could be reduced to just "write it up." I took a deep breath, then looked at him, raising one eyebrow—a move that had taken a lot of practice in front of a mirror.

"A little sketchy on the details there, Scooter."

Colin burst out laughing. Herbie looked confused.

Dan's enthusiasm held up. "I figured we'd want to work out the mystery together. Team bonding and all."

"You get away with a lot of shit just because you're good looking, don't you?"

"I hadn't thought of it that way. I thought I was charming." He gave me his most dazzling smile.

"Save it for the bored wives."

He shrugged. "I do get away with a lot of shit."

"No kidding. If I looked like you, I'd have a different woman every night," Herbie said.

We all looked at him.

"What? You guys are all on stage, getting the attention. I'm the nerdy sound guy. No one notices me."

Colin looked at Herbie, drawing a circle in the air to indicate his face and hair. "Oh yeah. Being onstage has made me a total chick magnet."

"Maybe if you used some product in your hair…" Dan started, trying to be helpful.

"Kids. Focus." I turned to Dan. "Using this to get material for a murder mystery show is not the worst idea in the world." Dan beamed at all of us, vindicated.

"But," I did my best Sean Bean impression: "One does not simply solve a murder."

"Well, that's why we need you, Kasey. You've got experience."

"Yeah, that Funniest Comics thing," Colin said.

"And the guy out in California."

I looked at Dan. "How do you know about that?"

"I worked with Luke Hallidade on a shoot in Orlando. We're both from Tampa, got talking. He said he did standup. One thing led to another."

I was starting to get a reputation. Great.

"What was the California thing? Herbie asked.

I sighed. "It was a comedy seminar. Luke was there. Anyway, this guy was blackmailing the woman who held the event and one of the instructors got murdered and it was all pretty ugly. I don't like to talk about it."

"Luke said you figured out who had attacked him at the Funniest Comics thing."

"Well, he would have told the cops once he was out of his coma."

"So, you solve crimes, Kasey." Herbie was looking at me with renewed interest. "Cool. We have a pro on the case."

I started to protest.

"Where do we begin? Dan asked.

They all looked at me. I sighed and took a sip of my coffee.

"It's probably going to be the husband." They looked disappoint-ed.

"But, to get background for the show, and mostly because we're stuck here anyway, let's see what we can work out." Their faces lit up again. "You are bored."

"To tell the truth, I don't think I'll ever forget opening that trunk and finding her body," Colin said. "I'd feel better knowing who did it."

"Especially since we can't go anywhere and there is a murderer among us," Dan pointed out.

We were silent. All of us were picturing Marie Janeé in that trunk.

"It was a lot of blood," Dan said. "She was kind of snooty, but she didn't deserve that."

We unconsciously nodded in agreement.

"Okay. We start with what we know. Which means I need to tell you something."

I filled them in on the encounter I had walked in on between Marie Janeé and Josh, right down to the lipstick on Josh's collar.

"God, I suck at this. I didn't notice that at all," Dan said.

Herbie looked around at us. "I *try* not to notice Josh at all." We laughed.

"I saw that, but I thought it was Laura's," Colin said.

"Different shade altogether. And I am sure Laura knew that."

"Maybe Laura killed her in a fit of jealous rage!" Dan was excited.

"Laura? Really?" Herbie scoffed.

"Good point. She is a bit mousy."

"I wouldn't say mousy," Herbie ventured. "She's just too nice."

"Maybe we should be writing this down," Colin suggested.

Before they could all look at me, I said, "You're all in charge of taking any notes you want." I had been in enough corporate meetings to know the men all expected "the girl" to be the secretary. Time to stop the generational sexism. "We should build a timeline, like the deputy said last night," I said to get them started.

"Good idea."

"That poor guy," Colin said.

"I don't envy him. He's got no support."

"Well, lucky for him, he's got us on the case!" Dan struck a pose.

"Somehow, I don't think he'll take that as good news." I had dealt with the police enough times to know they didn't like amateurs interfering. Actually, anyone who'd ever read a mystery knew that.

"I overheard a couple in the gift shop complaining that he was talking to everyone today but no one knew what time they were supposed to be there. Just groups of people scheduled by the hour."

"Good snooping, Herbie! That's the kind of intel we need." Dan was way too excited about this. I looked over at Colin and rolled my eyes. He grinned and shook his head.

Colin summed things up. "Okay, so he's interviewing everyone. That makes sense. Probably getting their movements and really, they're all going to say the same thing. 'We went from the show to the dining room.' Maybe a few went back to their rooms."

"I wonder if anyone saw Marie Janeé in the Ladies' Room. It was the one between the event room and the lobby. We're women. Someone would have ducked in there to check their makeup or to pee."

"How do we find out who, though?" Dan deflated a little.

"Maybe the same way Herbie picked up his info," Colin said. "We hang out in the gift shop or the bar—"

"It's a little early for the bar," Herbie said.

"Maybe not with this crowd," I countered. "There are some heavy drinkers in the group and I bet half of them were drinking bloody marys and mimosas at breakfast."

"Brunch, darling," Dan fawned. "They're all too classy for something as mundane as breakfast."

"I say we deploy Dan to talk up the ladies. We had to pull a few off him last night."

"Dan, Dan, the ladies' man," Herbie sing-songed.

"Some of those women are downright scary," Dan said.

"Yeah, but I noticed you didn't have a problem with some of the others," I said. "And they certainly didn't have a problem with you."

"Maybe Dan can work the bar, then. See if any of the women are in there," Colin suggested.

"Want to be my wing man?"

"I'd just scare them off. Take Herbie. He's kind of cute."

Herbie perked up. "Thanks, man."

"Kasey, you can work the men."

"Oh yeah. Great idea."

"We need to get information. Take one for the team. I am."

"Somehow, it's not the same for me, Dan."

He shrugged. I sighed.

"And where will you be, Colin?"

"I'll hit the gift shop, get a newspaper, and read it in the lobby. See if I can overhear anything."

"Maybe you should get a magazine. Otherwise, you'll be reading yesterday's paper. It'll look suspicious."

He looked at me.

"No ferry, no deliveries."

"Oh yeah." He shook his head and his curls shook for a half-second longer.

"What if Josh catches us out of our rooms?" Herbie asked.

"Right now, Josh is trying to stick us with the room bills. If we're paying for our rooms, we can go anywhere we want. We're guests."

"I really can't afford the room bill," Dan shook his head. "It's gotta be like $150 or something."

I didn't want to tell him it was more like $500 a night. No sense freaking him out.

"I'm sure they'll pay for our rooms. Don't worry about it." I gave him a reassuring nod.

Colin stood up. "Okay, let's get going. We can meet back up in the Staff Dining Room at 12:30."

"We can't really talk there," I said.

"No, but we can eat."

"Excellent point."

The guys left and I collected empty cups and threw them away. Including my own. I brushed my teeth, put on some tinted Burt's Bees, and made sure I had money in my pocket. Even orange juice at the bar was going to set me back and I wasn't sure if I could charge to my room.

It's Five O'Clock Somewhere

THERE WERE AROUND A dozen people in the bar. Apparently, there was a subset of people who didn't care if it was five o'clock anywhere. Edward and Irene were not present, but I figured they probably had room booze. Like me. No judgment. Well, a little judgment.

I sat at the far end of the bar so I could get a view of the door and most of the room. Dan and Herbie weren't here yet. I wondered if there was more than one bar. The bartender stepped right up to get my order. He laid down a coaster and a black cocktail napkin with the resort's logo embossed in gold. Swanky. I played it safe with an orange juice.

"I can make that a mimosa for you," he offered with a rather charming smile.

"It's a little early for me. But I was tired of looking at the walls of my room. So."

"Got ya." He returned with my juice almost immediately. He scanned the room to see if anyone needed a drink. People seemed to be more interested in talking than drinking. I looked around to see if I recognized anyone from last night's audience. I wished I had paid more attention. But there was a certain sameness to the people. They were all dressed in casual, but expensive clothes. They were all well-groomed. Most of the women had the same shade of ash-blonde hair. Shoulder length. Expensively cut and styled. I turned back to the bartender.

"I guess I don't quite fit in with this crowd."

"The red hair does stand out," He leaned in and whispered, "Stepford Wives."

"Thank you! They're kind of scary."

He laughed.

"How long are you staying with us?"

"I was supposed to leave this morning."

"You're stuck with us. Well, that's a nice thing for me."

I was sure that was part of his guest patter. But it dawned on me that the staff was just as stuck as we were.

"You're stuck here, too."

"Most of the full-time staff live in staff quarters. It's easier to put us up than to ask people to take the ferry back and forth to work every day. Most of the bigger resorts do this."

"You mean more expensive resorts."

"That, too."

A waitress came up to the service area, unloaded a few dirty glasses, and ordered two G & Ts. My stomach lurched just thinking about gin, never mind gin at this hour. I watched him rinse out the dirty glasses and put them in a rack, then dry his hands on a cloth he had tucked in his belt. The waitress delivered the drinks to one of the tables with a professional smile, and did a visual check of the occupied tables. Efficient. She went through a doorway at the back of the bar which I assumed led to the kitchen.

The bartender came back. "I'm Vitor, by the way. So, you don't have to say 'Hey you' when you want another."

I smiled. "Kasey. So, you don't have to call me ma'am."

"I do *not* make that mistake. If a lady is a hundred and eight, I'm still going to call her miss."

I pretended to look around the room, then asked casually, "How are people doing today? After the, um, incident, last night?"

His eyes clouded over. "That's a very sad thing."

"Yes."

He recovered a bit. "There's a lot of alcohol going up to the rooms. And the dining room. Honestly, I usually don't have this many people in here this early."

"Anesthesia. Do you think they all knew the victim?"

"The ones who knew her are the worst."

I looked at him more closely. "How do you mean?"

"Probably women just being catty. The men, too, for that matter. She was very beautiful."

"So, you had met her?"

"Yes. She and her husband come here often."

I nodded. "Happily married, then?"

"For the economic strata, sure." He shifted away and pretended to wipe down an area of the bar that was already clean. He was taking deep breaths and swallowing hard. The waitress came back through the door with a tray of Danish pastries, cut in smaller pieces like appetizers. She set it down in front of a couple who had half-full champagne flutes in front of them. She picked up a bottle from a stainless steel wine cooler and topped up their glasses. Then she made another sweep of her tables, taking orders.

Herbie and Dan walked in and sat at one of the tables, studiously ignoring me. *Are we pretending not to know each other? Because we all did a show together last night. I'm pretty sure people will recognize us. Well, maybe not Herbie. Nobody notices the sound guy.*

The waitress went back to delivering drinks and took their order. I had finished my orange juice. A minute or so later, Vitor was back, smile in place.

"Another?"

"Sure, why not? I had a rough night."

"Just don't get too crazy."

He returned with a fresh glass and whisked the old one away. I was the only one at his bar. He was too professional to stand around doing nothing and I was very sure staff members weren't allowed to look at their cell phones while on duty. Not that it would have done much good. Cell towers were down, too. He came back to my end of the bar.

A couple of women walked in together. They looked vaguely familiar. I was pretty sure that one had been hitting on Dan last night. I watched as they chose the table next to Dan and Herbie. *Yep.*

"How long do you think this storm will last?" I asked.

"It's slow moving, but it should blow out sometime after midnight. Don't worry, you're not stuck forever."

"I guess there are worse things than being stuck in an upscale resort."

Just then all the lights went out. A couple of people gave little screams, then someone giggled nervously. *Me and my big mouth.*

"Don't worry," Vitor said in a loud voice. "It's just the storm. We have back up generators. And," he paused for effect, "more important, I don't need electricity to pour your drinks."

People laughed, but they were still on edge. About thirty seconds later, the lights came back on. Not quite all of them, but enough.

"Not your first rodeo," I observed.

"We evacuate for hurricanes, but tropical storms do more than enough damage. The resort has backups for everything. We can run seven days on the generators. After that, it gets a bit ugly."

Irene came in, alone. She spotted me at the bar.

"Hello Christmas Carol!" Irene greeted me. I was afraid she was going to come in for the two-cheek air kiss. "What are you drinking?"

"Just orange juice. Don't want to get on Santa's naughty list."

"I try to stay on Santa's naughty list. It's more fun." She looked at the bar then looked around the room. "Carol, come sit with me."

Drunks hate to drink alone

Apparently, she had forgotten my real name. I was Carol to her. Fine. "Happy to."

Irene looked over at Vitor. "How about some bloody marys? Yes?"

She was buying. Or rather, Edward was.

Vitor looked at me and I made a motion to keep my drink light.

"You get settled and I'll bring them over."

Irene practically pulled me off the bar stool. We sat at a nearby table while Vitor made our drinks. The waitress started to pick up the drinks but he waved her off. He flipped up the counter by the service station and brought out the tray himself. He set out the drinks, and winked at me as he put mine down.

Irene raised her glass. "To getting off this island!" We clinked glasses. I took a careful sip of my bloody mary. It was a virgin. *Well done, Vitor.* I had seen Irene in action; there was no way I could hold my own against her.

"Not quite the company party you expected, is it?" I said. Might as well start with the obvious.

"A horrible thing," Irene said. "And then Edward and I were interrogated by that Barney Fife."

"We were questioned first thing this morning," I said. I could almost see her wondering why we got to go first. "Since we were the ones who found her body, I guess he wanted to get that set down first."

"Oh, that's right. So gruesome." Irene's eyes sparkled.

"We're all pretty shaken up."

"We were thinking it was someone after her jewelry. I was terrified they'd be after me next." She gave a short laugh and sucked down a substantial level of bloody mary.

"Was she robbed?"

"What? Oh. No. The deputy said she still had her jewelry."

I nodded.

"But you can see why I'd be worried. Edward buys me such nice things." She held out her wrist, which was graced with a gorgeous, modern ruby and diamond bracelet. "Early Christmas present."

Bully for Edward. "I think it's better to be on Edward's nice list than Santa's."

"Oh, I'm definitely on Edward's *naughty* list." She laughed and gave me a big wink. Judging from the diamond ring and wedding band, I had to admit that being on Edward's naughty list paid off better than Santa's nice list.

I noticed her bloody mary was down by two-thirds. I drank more of mine to make it look like I was keeping pace. "So, you just met with Deputy Fletcher?"

"It was humiliating. Being questioned over the murder of that little tra—uh, Marie Janeé. Why would we want to harm her?"

"I'm sure he's just trying to determine everyone's whereabouts at this point."

She shrugged. "I guess. We went right from the show into dinner," Irene said, a little too quickly. My BS detector dinged.

I looked around the bar as if I was worried someone might overhear me. I leaned in and whispered, "I saw her in the hall, going into the ladies' room."

Irene's eyes widened. "I was *in* the ladies' room when she walked in."

Bingo. I knew she'd have to one-up me.

"Oh my God! Did she say anything?"

"Not really. Just hello. I was fixing my lipstick. She ducked into a stall pretty quickly and I left." She thought back. "Her lipstick was a mess."

"I saw that!"

Irene looked over at Vitor behind the bar. "Two guesses as to who's responsible for that."

This time I didn't have to pretend. "Vitor?" I whispered.

Irene's eyes were glittering at this point, and it wasn't the alcohol. "She and Vitor had a thing before she met Stephen. He was heartbroken when she dumped him for Stephen. I tried to console him, poor dear."

I played along. "I wouldn't mind consoling him."

"Amen, sister."

I had a thought. "Did Marie Janeé work here?"

"Oh, no. She and Vitor worked at a private business club up in Tampa. The company holds monthly meetings there. Now that I think about it, he left the club shortly after Marie Janeé and Stephen got together. Frankly, I was surprised to see him here."

"You should never date people at work."

"Not unless he's the boss and you can get him to marry you." Irene raised an eyebrow. She looked towards the service end of the bar. Vitor was on his way. He came by and dropped off another round without being asked. He took away Irene's empty glass and returned to the bar. I waited until he was back at the bar.

"Did you tell the deputy all this?" I asked in a low voice.

"Oh, dear God, no. We don't want to get involved. Edward said to answer the questions but not volunteer any information. Don't ask, don't tell," she finished brightly.

I was very sure that wasn't what the phrase meant. I wondered who else knew something and wasn't telling. I changed tacks. "Have you talked to Mr. Vashon since it happened?"

"No, but Edward and Trip—he's the second-in-command—are meeting with him now. Edward talked to him last night. That deputy has put Stephen through the wringer."

From what I had seen of Deputy Fletcher, I very much doubted it. Maybe when you reached a certain level of wealth or power, any question seems like an attack.

"I can't imagine what he's going through. He was such a good sport about playing Scrooge."

She nodded.

"I guess Mr. Vashon is going to need some time off after this."

"We have a two week break at the holidays anyway. But that's not until the twentieth. Everything is upside down at the moment. Marie Janeé's murder threw a monkey wrench into our agenda for last night. Stephen was going to make a big announcement, but he didn't want to make it without Marie Janeé being there."

"What was the announcement?"

"I have no idea."

I tried to think of something else to say. "What do Trip and Judy think of all this? Will it affect the company?"

"Not unless it turns out Stephen killed her." Irene's laugh was more of a short bark. "I'm kidding, of course. Everyone knows Stephen was totally besotted with her." She took a long draw of her drink.

"Well, she seemed to be very much in love with him, too." I said. "They were holding hands when they came in to meet us before the show. I thought it was cute."

Irene huffed but she didn't say anything.

"How long had they been married?"

"About two years," Irene said. "Apparently it was a whirlwind romance."

"Must have been a hell of a wedding."

"Hardly," Irene sniffed. "They got married on some island in the Caribbean. On the beach. Nobody even knew Stephen was dating anyone. Then, he casually mentions at a meeting that he got married."

"Well, I guess it doesn't really affect the company, does it? It's not like she works there."

"Stephen is the majority shareholder. So, by extension, if anything happens to him, she's the majority shareholder." Irene shuddered.

"Needless to say, she may be equipped for a lot of things, but not running a fifty-million-dollar corporation."

"But Stephen looks to be in good shape. And there must be buy-out clauses and things like that." I hoped I wasn't being too interested, but Irene jumped on it.

"That's what I said to Edward. If anything happened to Stephen, she would have taken the money and run back to her flavor of the month."

Whoa.

"Marie Janeé wasn't faithful?"

"Puhleeze." Irene's bloody mary was heading towards refill territory.

"Do you think she and Vitor still had a thing?"

"Oh, no. Well, maybe."

"If she was cheating, maybe Stephen was, too."

Irene considered this. "Well, they all do. Even Edward wanders. But then, I've been known to wander myself." She gave a tight smile. I wondered how much consoling she'd like to give Vitor.

"Maybe he and Marie Janeé were going to divorce."

"Doubtful. Stephen thought he had finally found the one."

"So, this wasn't Stephen's first marriage?"

"Marie Janeé was his third," Irene offered. No judgment in her voice on that.

I felt my eyebrows shoot up and tried to get them back under control. "I guess that's pretty common these days," I smiled at her. "The first divorce is because you married too young, the second is the rebound mistake, usually short. And third time's a charm."

"That's what Stephen said about Marie Janeé. I think he truly was in love with her. She may have loved him, but she loved his money more. It was pretty obvious." For the first time, I saw some sympathy come into Irene's eyes.

She looked at my glass. "Another?"

"Not for me, thank you. I better get going. Thanks for the drinks."

We said our good byes and I went over to the bar to clear my tab.

"What do I owe you?"

Vitor laughed. "Two orange juices? On the house."

I noticed he was setting up another bloody mary.

"She can put them away."

"Good choice to not try to keep up."

I nodded. I put a five-dollar bill on the bar as a thanks.

"I'll probably see you later," I said.

"I'll keep an eye out." He gave me his professional smile and flipped up the service bar gate to deliver Irene's drink.

I kind of hated what I was going to do next, but it had to be done.

The Part Where the Cop Tells Me to Butt Out

I WENT THROUGH THE lobby but didn't see Colin. I turned the corner and headed down to the event room where Deputy Fletcher was set up. No one was in the chairs outside the room. I opened the door and peeked in. There was a well-dressed couple sitting in front of the deputy. He with the white hair, she with the requisite shoulder-length ash-blonde. The deputy looked up at the click of the door. I gave a little wave and he nodded. The couple turned to look at me.

"Sorry to interrupt," I started.

"Give us a couple of minutes and then I can see you," Deputy Fletcher said.

I backed out and sat on a chair. I didn't have to wait long. Deputy Fletcher escorted them out and beckoned me in. I followed him to the table and took a seat.

"Did you remember something?" he asked.

"No, but I found out something and I think it might be important. You might know already…" I hesitated. Irene obviously wasn't the only person who knew Vitor and Marie Janeé back in the day. "I was talking to Irene in the bar…"

"Irene who?"

I had no idea. "She's married to Edward. I don't know their last name."

He scanned his list. "Winship. Okay."

"Anyway, Irene said that she saw Marie Janeé in the ladies' room last night."

"Convenient for you."`

"What?"

"So far, you were the last person to see Marie Janeé alive. Now you volunteer that someone else saw her after you. Convenient."

My eyes widened. "I'm a suspect?"

"Would you like to confess now and make my job easier?" He said it in a half-joking manner, but I had a feeling that he would be very happy if I did.

"No. Sorry."

"Didn't think so." He let out a sigh. "What else did Irene say?"

I related what Irene had told me, about Marie Janeé and Vitor being an item; the club up in Tampa, and that if anything happened to Stephen Vashon, Marie Janeé would inherit the majority shares of the company. I wrapped it up. "So, a lot of people with a lot of motives."

He had been taking notes. I tried to read the other papers in front of him upside down. It was the list of people he was interviewing, with check marks next to the people he had already spoken with.

"I'm not really a suspect, am I?"

"You were one of the last people to see Marie Janeé, and then, by your own admission, you went up to your room, washed up, and changed your clothes."

I blinked. Several times. "I was just doing what I always do after a show."

"So, if I asked to see your costume it wouldn't have any blood on it."

"You're welcome to check it."

"I already have."

"What? Can you do that without a warrant?"

"The company paid for your rooms. Technically, I just needed their permission. I went in with the manager. We only checked your costume, the bottoms of your booties, and we left."

"And did you check anyone else's room?" I was pissed.

"I am not going to give you the details of my investigation, but yours was not the only room we checked."

I felt marginally better. But I was definitely checking my room when I got back to see if anything else was touched.

"You have good taste in scotch."

"Josh was very clear that we wouldn't have bar privileges. It was my little way of..." I trailed off. "Petty, I know."

"I guess the 'no bar privileges' rule has been thrown out the window."

"It pretty much went out the window last night. Colin and I stopped in for a drink and no one threw us out."

He looked at his list and softly said, "Bourbon."

"You checked Colin's room."

"You four found the body. We checked all your rooms."

"Great. Did you check Josh and Laura's?"

"No. They were in the banquet room." He looked at his list. "So far, everyone was in the banquet room. No one went back to their rooms. No one went to the rest rooms."

"Except Irene went to the ladies' room."

He looked at me. "People lie to me all day long. These people lie for sport. Between last night and this morning, it's like they all agreed they went as a group from the event room to the banquet room." He threw his pen down on the table. "You were my best suspect."

"Sorry to disappoint."

"Well, you're still in the mix."

"Thanks."

"How did you happen to be drinking early in the day with Irene Winship?"

I squirmed a bit. "I was having an orange juice in the bar…"

"All. Day. Long."

Damn his BS detector is good.

"We're stuck here for another day. Nothing to do. We're thinking about writing a murder mystery show so we decided to kind of check things out and see if we could—"

"See if you could solve the murder? Really? This isn't a game."

"We know that. We found the body."

"This is the part where I tell you not to interfere."

"I might just as easily point out that you have over fifty suspects and no one to help you. Unless you count Ray, the security guy who just about fainted when he saw the body." I didn't mention that we just about fainted, too.

"I appreciate your telling me what you learned, but I really need you four to stay clear."

"So, if the guys learned anything this morning, you don't want to know?"

He sighed. "You hear anything important, yes, tell me. You're supposed to do that anyway. But don't go looking for trouble. I've got one dead woman. I don't need any more bodies."

"Understood."

I walked out of the room with my emotions churning. I was pissed off that my room had been searched. And that I'd been told to butt out after I turned up more information than he had. But I also knew he was right about more bodies turning up; one murder had a way of leading to the next. It's like the murderer thinks, 'In for a penny, in for a pound.' If whoever murdered Marie Janeé sensed we were getting close to finding them, we'd all be in danger. I knew that, but the guys didn't. We were putting ourselves at risk. What had seemed like a harmless way to kill time could very well kill us. Deputy Fletcher was right: Time to stop nosing around.

I HAD BROUGHT A book with me for reading material. And my laptop. I could do some writing. Maybe being cooped up in my room for the day wouldn't be so bad.

I walked over to the gift shop to see if anything there would make a nice addition to my room food stock. I picked up some Lorna Doone cookies, not because I needed them, but because I can't resist them. Every time I eat them, I do the old Three Stooges line: "Hiya Lorna. How ya doin?" It makes me laugh. I'm a simple girl.

I debated potato chips but figured my bag of kettle corn would take care of any salt-crunch cravings. I added a six pack of Sam Adams Boston Lager, partly because I was surprised to find it, partly to have something for the guys to drink. My total came to just under twenty dollars. The six pack of cookies was not the bank-breaker. The fifty percent markup on the beer was. Eeesh.

I went back up to my room and put the beer in the mini-fridge. By then it was almost 12:30, so I headed down to the staff dining room. Colin was already there.

I went through the line and got a hot open face turkey sandwich with a side of crinkle cut fries. I figured I'd go back for dessert. I could probably eat chocolate cake every day of the week. Here I'd get to test my theory. I grabbed two bottled waters—the virgin marys were a bit salty.

Dan and Herbie came in as I was sitting down. They made their way through the line and joined us.

Dan bit into a French fry. "At least the food here is good."

Herbie nodded.

Colin asked quietly, "Did anybody get anything?"

"Boy howdy," I said. They looked at me. "Later." I looked at them. "How about you?"

"Dan got hit on."

"Hot stuff," Colin said.

"She was at least twice my age. It was icky."

"I don't know Dan, older women, hitting their stride," I teased.

"Reverse the sexes," Dan said flatly.

Oops. "Yeah. Point taken. Sorry."

"I see a lot of that where I work," Colin said.

"Where do you work?" I asked.

"USF, Tampa. It's totally against the rules, but some of the male professors manipulate the students." He paused, thinking. "Of course, it goes the other way, too. Some of these, well girls, really, are pretty forward."

"So do you get hit on?" Herbie asked. He sounded a little incredulous.

Colin looked amused. "Believe it or not, even I am occasionally hit on."

"You're a professor at USF?" I asked.

"Yes. Physics."

We all sat back in our chairs. Colin looked at us.

"What did you think I do?"

"Not physics," Dan said.

"Hadn't given it much thought," Herbie added.

"We have worked together for months and we know nothing about each other." I stated the obvious.

This gave us a chance to talk about something besides the murder. One good thing was coming out of this nightmare of a weekend; we were getting to know each other. A few employees came and went while we were there. They looked over, but no one approached us. I figured a good percentage of the employees were serving up lunch in the main dining room. We ate quickly, but none of us passed on dessert. I got a coffee to go with my cake. We put our plates in the dish bins that were off to one side and headed back to our rooms. Josh would be pleased.

Apparently, Yes. Josh Was Raised By Wolves

I JUST HAD TIME to go to the bathroom and brush my teeth before there was a knock on the door. I opened the door, expecting one of the guys. It was Laura.

"Hey, what's up?"

"Can I come in?"

"Sure, of course." I stepped aside so she could come in.

She took a seat at the table set-up. I glanced around the room, a little grateful that I had put my bottle of scotch in the closet. No need for Josh to know we were actively circumventing his directives.

"Josh talked to the hotel manager and he got our rooms comped for the night."

"That's good news. I'm surprised he didn't want to tell us that himself," I said.

"He's in a meeting right now."

I waited to see if she was going to tell me who he was meeting with, but she didn't volunteer the information.

"You and the guys are getting along okay?"

"Sure. We're actually getting to know each other, which is nice." I looked at her. "Why?"

She plunged ahead. "So, the deal Josh made with the hotel manager is that we put on a show for the employees tonight. Evening really. At 5:00."

"We do the show?" I shrugged. "No biggie."

"Do you think the guys will mind?"

"Not when I tell them how much the hotel rooms are here."

She laughed. "Yeah. I mean, really, the company should pick up our hotel rooms, but with everything that's happened…"

I tried to imagine Josh having the emotional IQ to pick up on that. I couldn't. Laura probably had said something about it.

"What about the props? They're police evidence right now."

"I have the hats in my room, and we can use a tablecloth or sheet as a cape. The cape ended up in the prop box. Even if it wasn't ruined, I don't think anyone would want to touch it, much less wear it."

I thought back to finding the body. I hadn't noticed the cape, but it could have been underneath her. I was pretty focused on that icicle.

Laura was still talking. "I'm redoing the cue cards this afternoon. But we're going to need to scrounge around to get the rest of the props."

"I take it that is our job."

"If you can? I mean, there's four of you and you're pretty resourceful."

"Do you have the list?"

She handed me a sheet. Silence hung between us.

"Something else?" I asked.

"So, Josh was thinking maybe you could do a bonus comedy set for the VashTech people after their dinner tonight."

My jaw dropped. "What?"

"You know, maybe cheer people up."

"No!"

She didn't respond.

"Do you even need me to tell you why? Really?"

Her eyes filled up with tears. "I told him it was a bad idea."

"It's tacky as hell. Insensitive…"

"I know. He told me to go sell it to you."

"Tell him no sale. And to not even mention it to the client. Was he raised by wolves?"

"Sometimes, he just doesn't think."

"This might be in the top five of his all-time bad ideas. We'll do the show for the employees. Where are we doing that?"

"The staff dining room. The catering department is going to clear a little stage area."

That wasn't a problem. We'd done the show in living rooms.

"Okay. I'll get the guys and we'll see what we can scrounge up for props. I don't think we'll find a rubber chicken, though."

She nodded and stood up to leave. "Can I tell Josh you're thinking about the comedy set?"

"NO! Hard no."

"Josh thinks you owe him for throwing him under the bus to the deputy."

I looked at her. Was she really backing Josh on that?

"You mean my telling the deputy that Josh was all over Marie Janeé? And that she rejected him?"

"Josh said she came on to *him*."

"And you believe that?" I looked her straight in the eyes. She squirmed.

"Laura, I'm sorry, but he was definitely coming on to her. He had her pinned against the wall. She kneed him in the groin."

She said nothing.

"Look at her. Look at him. Hell, look at Stephen Vashon, look at Josh."

She sighed. "I didn't really believe him."

I nodded.

"Sometimes with Josh, it's just easier to agree."

"Josh likes to get his way," I said.

"He really wants you to do the comedy show."

"You're going to have to explain to him why the idea alone is tacky."

"He's going to tell me I'm useless."

"Tell him you had to talk me into doing the show for the employees. You're batting 500."

I opened the door for her. It was like she was marching towards the firing squad. I had no doubt Josh would give her a hard time; it's what he did.

Laura's self-esteem must be pretty low to put up with that. But she probably wouldn't appreciate my telling her that.

I flipped over the latch to leave my door slightly ajar. The guys would be here any minute. I looked over the prop list and shuddered when I saw the icicle listed. We used it for a throwaway Bugs Bunny "What's up, Scrooge?" line. I wondered what we could substitute. Maybe just cut the line.

Herbie was the first through the door. He had beer with him.

"We might want to go light on the beer right now," I said.

"Why?"

"I'll tell you when everyone gets here."

Colin and Dan showed up together. Dan closed the door behind them.

"Beer, great!"

Herbie looked over at me.

"Not quite yet. A couple of things," I began.

"Yeah, what did you find out?"

"I'll do that second. First, we're singing for our supper, or our sleep in this case. Josh negotiated a deal with the hotel: We're doing the show for the employees tonight. Actually, around 5:00. So, we're going to need to gather props. Herbie, you've got access to your sound equipment, right?"

"Yeah, they sent it up to my room last night. I had to convince the security guy, then the hotel manager, and then the deputy that it wasn't used in the crime. But at least I got it."

"That's a start."

"What did you learn?" Colin asked.

"It might not matter." I told them that Deputy Fletcher wanted us to butt out. "And he's right. If we did find out something, it could put us all in danger."

"He searched our rooms?" Herbie was indignant.

"He says he just checked our costumes." I shrugged.

"Can he do that without a warrant?" Dan asked.

"That was my first question. Apparently, yes because we didn't pay for our rooms. He got permission from, I guess Stephen Vashon."

"I'm really not good with that," Colin said.

"On the plus side, he didn't find any blood-soaked clothes, so we're semi in the clear."

"No kidding," Herbie said. "Figures we're the first people they look at. Just because we're not high-falutin' executives."

"That and we were the ones who found her body," I pointed out.

"It would serve him right if we solved the case." Dan was getting excited again. "We could show him up."

I knew exactly where he was coming from. He had watched way too many movies. Dan had already cast himself as the hero in solving this murder. He'd probably already worked out the fight scenes in his head. I wondered if he even knew how much real punches hurt. I did.

"Dan, in the movies, the hero doesn't die. But real-life murderers don't care if you're the hero. You're just someone who is in the way. Someone murdered Marie Janeé and they will do anything to make sure they aren't discovered. And if we keep poking around, they might decide one or all of us is in the way."

The guys were silent. Then Colin spoke.

"They might decide that anyway."

"What?"

"You were one of the last people to see Marie Janeé alive. We found the body. What's to say the murderer isn't watching us right now, seeing how much we know?"

"But we really don't know anything," I countered.

"But the murderer doesn't know that. The murderer knows who we are. We don't know who the murderer is."

Dan grinned. "So, really, we need to keep investigating to protect ourselves."

Herbie got on board. "We'll just be real subtle so Deputy Fletcher doesn't find out what we're doing."

"Besides, he's the one who said if you hear anything, you need to tell him," Colin said. "I'd say the man is sending mixed signals."

I sighed inwardly. "We do need to go out looking for props, so I guess we can try to pick up on something."

"Yeah!" Dan and Colin high-fived.

"Let me tell you what I got from Irene."

I told them about Marie Janeé and Vitor, the bartender. And that her marriage to Stephen happened at lightning speed. "None of the exec wives liked her. She was his third wife."

"She represented the next round of trophy wives," Dan said. We all looked at him.

"The women hitting on me were all in their forties. Or thereabouts. Their husbands are all at least ten years older, some more than that."

"Vitor called them Stepford Wives."

Dan went on. "They're hitting the same age the first wives were when they got traded in. And most of them know it."

"Wow. Kind of sexist, isn't it? Are you saying all of those women married for money?"

"Not all. But most. I get hit on a lot. Mostly it's bored housewives who like to brag to their girlfriends about their, um, extracurricular activities."

"I always assumed it was the men that cheated," I said.

"Oh, they're cheating, too." Dan was matter-of-fact. "Sometimes the wives are cheating just to get back at their husbands." He looked kind of sad.

"Wow." Herbie looked stupefied. I was right there with him.

"I feel so naïve. Everyone is cheating?"

"Just in some social circles. They think they're sophisticated. This is one of those circles."

"Eww."

"Yeah."

"Wait a minute!" Herbie said. "Was *that* what Sasha meant when she was talking about the grand prize?"

Colin and I looked over at Dan. He threw his hands up in the air. "Duh, Herbie. Yeah."

"And you're the grand prize?" Herbie asked.

"This weekend. It will be someone else at their next corporate retreat. The bartender, the personal trainer, whoever."

"How do you know this stuff?" I asked. I was trying to wrap my head around it.

Dan blushed. "I, uh, sometimes work as a 'walker' for older ladies."

"A what?"

"Walker. Escort. No sex!" He answered our unasked question. "I mean, man, most are like my grandmother's age! It's just that wealthy people go to a lot of charity events and it's always couples. A lot of older women are divorced or widowed and they need a dinner partner. Tall, young."

"Good-looking," Colin put in.

Dan ducked his head a bit. "Some like to dance, which I can do. We make conversation, dance. I show interest only in them."

"What does that pay?" Herbie asked.

"A couple of hundred dollars a night." He brightened. "Plus, you get dinner usually." I got the feeling Dan was more in it for the food than the money.

"So, you're a male escort." I tried to sound casual. We really were getting to know each other. Maybe too well.

"Well, in a way, yeah. But these women aren't out for sex, just someone to be on their arm. Anyway, I've got my regulars and they talk. One lady in particular, Vivian, real nice, she's widowed. She told me about the games the younger women play. Warned me, basically. Which was super-helpful. She was the one that told me if I could dance—the ballroom stuff—I would get requested more. So, I took lessons. And she helped me practice. She loves to dance." He looked around. I'm sure all of our jaws were hanging open.

"Anyway, that's how I know about the game."

Herbie blinked a few times.

Colin was the first to speak. "Alrighty, then."

"Marie Janeé represented the next... wave of wives?" I wondered how this fit into her being murdered. If it did at all. Then I had another thought. "Do you think Vitor was a grand prize at one point?"

Dan shrugged. "The bartender? Possibly. Probably. This company has had events here before."

"And Irene said Vitor—and Marie Janeé —used to work at a business club in Tampa. He might have been the prize there."

Colin was thinking along a different track. "Third round of wives. Does Vashon have any kids from his previous marriages?"

"Why?" Herbie asked.

"The second round of wives don't want to be replaced because they'll lose their meal tickets." He made air quotes with his hands. "If he has adult kids, maybe they didn't like this third wife coming in and maybe making off with their inheritance."

"I didn't think of that. Damn."

"So, maybe that's something we should check on."

"Maybe. A lot of times the kids will work in the company. Maybe we can find out. Somehow." Dan had started to get excited, then caught himself.

"Do you think the bartender might have killed her? Maybe he was jealous that she dumped him for a rich guy." Herbie looked at us.

It was a good motive. I thought back to Vitor's reaction to just mentioning Marie Janeé. Had he been trying not to cry or fighting down a panic attack?

"We need a cocktail shaker for the show. I'll go down and see if I can borrow one from him. Maybe I can chat him up." I was the obvious one to talk to him but I didn't know how I was going to broach the subject. Subtlety is not my strong suit.

We divvied up the short list of props. I looked at 'Icicle' on the list. "I think we need to cut the icicle joke for tonight's show."

"It's the employees. Do you think they know?" Herbie asked.

"They probably know more than we do," Colin said. "Herbie, maybe you can talk to some of the employees—go into the staff dining room and ask about where to set up your equipment, where you can plug in, all that. Just hang out and be chatty."

"I can do that."

"I didn't get anything sitting in the lobby," Colin continued. "I'm going to try the business center. I have papers to grade and I can sit in a corner and look harmless if anyone comes in."

"Sounds good."

"That leaves me with the ladies, again," Dan said.

"You are so good at it." There was only a little snark in Colin's voice.

"My face is my fortune."

"Well, for most of the wives, their faces are their fortunes, too. You have something to bond over." I stood up. "We know a little more than we did before. Let's not assume anything, but try to find out whether Stephen has grown kids, if any of the employees have heard anything…

and, I guess we shouldn't get stuck on any one theory. Keep an open mind. The show is at 5:00 which means we need to be down there in costume by 4:30. Don't forget to find the props, too. We'll need to meet back here and make sure we have everything."

I held the door and made a swooshing motion to usher them out. The beer was on the table, forgotten. I put it in the room's mini-fridge, next to the Sam Adams, brushed my hair, and headed out.

Can Anyone Spare a Rubber Chicken?

"Ah, you couldn't stay away!" Vitor greeted me.

"I am on a mission." I explained that we were doing the show for the employees and asked if I could borrow a martini shaker.

"Sure thing." He reached under the bar and brought one out. "Just bring it back."

"No worries. And thanks." I looked around the bar; there were fewer people than earlier.

"Where did everyone go?"

"It's afternoon nap time. Juice?"

"Sure, thanks."

He poured my orange juice and set it down. "Thanks for virginizing my bloody marys. Irene can put them back."

"They all can. That's why mid-afternoons are so nice here." He smiled.

"Irene said that you worked with Marie Janeé up in Tampa. Her death must be hitting you hard."

He nodded. "I'm sure that's not all Irene said."

"Said you two were an item."

He nodded. "We were. But Marie Janeé was heading for bigger and better things. She was pretty honest about that."

"Was she already Marie Janeé back then?"

He gave a short laugh. "Oh, yeah. We joked about it, a bit. But she said, 'Sure, you've already got a sexy name. Mine is barely middle class.' She was always looking to move up."

"Mary Jane. Plain Jane. Yeah, I can see why she would change it, especially if she was doing shows."

"Yes. Her stage name. Is Kasey your stage name?"

"Not really. I've been called Kasey since I was a kid. My real first name is Katherine." I didn't want to explain to him that my middle name was Catherine. It got old.

"Ah, Katherine is a very strong name. Katherine the Great."

"Kasey is more user-friendly." A thought occurred to me. "So, you knew Marie Janeé from before. And probably, most of the executives and their wives knew her from Tampa."

"Yes."

"Did anyone else here at the resort work with you two up in Tampa?"

He thought for a minute. "No. I shifted down here after Marie Janeé and I broke up. Well, after she came back from a getaway vacation with Stephen that turned into marriage."

"Yeah, I guess that would split you up." There was a short silence. "She was still dating you when she married Stephen?"

"Yes."

"Kind of a shock."

"More of a kick in the teeth. She told me she was going to the Keys with the girls." He looked sad more than angry.

"Ouch."

"She should have just been honest with me. It's not like I didn't know she was looking to move up." He was silent for a few seconds, thinking back. Then he grinned. "Created quite a stir among the Stepford Wives when the CEO married the help."

"I bet." I had already sensed that rift.

"So, even though she was not working there any more, it was... how did she put it? Uncomfortable for me to be working where their company held so many meetings."

"Excuse you."

"Stephen got me a job here. I can't complain. The weather is better. Usually. I get room and board. I'm paid well. The tips are ridiculously good. And once or twice a year I see Marie Janeé Vashon. And I keep my distance."

"Does it hurt to see her?"

"No. We move on." He paused. "Still, for her to be murdered like that, that's just too horrible. She was a climber, yes. But we both wanted something better for ourselves. She found a way out before I did, that's all. And she looked happy. Happy enough at least."

"So, are you looking to marry well?" I said it with a smile.

"After the time I have spent watching these husbands and wives, I think I have redefined my idea of marrying well."

"Are they all unhappy?"

"No. In fact, most of them are fairly content. But they're all..." he searched for words. "They're all on edge, waiting for the boom to drop. The wives worry about being replaced by someone younger. Hell, the men worry about being replaced by someone younger—on the job, at least. Everyone is watching everyone else. They socialize, make jokes, talk. They even like each other to a certain extent. But they don't *trust* each other."

"Bartenders really do know everything."

He smiled. "That's because alcohol loosens tongues. Everyone talks to me. A good bartender is like a priest. You tell me your sins and I smile, tell you it will all be okay, and then I never mention them again."

"Has anyone confessed to murdering Marie Janeé?"

"That's a no. I'm a good bartender. But like each other, they only trust me so far."

I laughed.

A manager of some sort came through the door from the kitchen.

"Vitor, the deputy wants to talk to you. I'll take over."

He looked at me.

"I had my turn this morning," I said with a shrug, playing it down.

He squared his shoulders and nodded.

"Break a leg."

He hung his towel on a hook and left the bar. I was pretty sure the deputy was going to give him a close look. Ex-boyfriends. Husbands. Top suspects when a woman is murdered. Vitor had been pretty open with me about their relationship. *Would a murderer do that? And here I sit like a dope, chatting him up.*

A couple I didn't recognize wandered into the bar and sat at a table. The manager looked around for the waitress, then realized she was probably on break. He grabbed a tray added a few napkins and bar coasters and hustled over to them. He checked the few other tables on the way back, made a bit of conversation, smiling. He returned and busied himself making drinks, served them, picked up a few empties. He washed out the glasses, humming a bit to himself. Then he came over to check on me.

"I'm Tom. Vitor's on a little break. Are you doing okay over here?"

"I'm fine. I really just came in to borrow this shaker." I held it up. "We're doing a show for the employees in a couple of hours."

"You're in the show? That's great. We're looking forward to it."

"For real, or are you just being polite?"

"For real. Cable's out."

I laughed.

"What's the show?"

"A take-off on Dickens' *A Christmas Carol*. Funny. Usually."

"That'll be great."

"We're collecting props. I don't suppose you would know where I could get a length of chain, do you?"

His smile broadened. "As a matter of fact, I do. When Vitor gets back, I'll take care of you. What happened to your props?"

I looked around and lowered my voice. "They're in police evidence."

"Oh, man." Then he lowered his voice to match mine. "Wait—are you one of the people who found Mrs. Vashon's body?"

I nodded.

"Sorry. That must have been rough."

"It wasn't good. We're not supposed to talk about it." I paused. "But you know about it."

"I'm the F&B Manager. Food and Beverage. Upper management all knows about it. And frankly. I'm sure the entire staff knows. No secrets here."

"Did the deputy already talk with you?"

"Yes. Basically, just asked me where I was between 8:00 and 9:45 last night. Which was easy because we were working the banquet, the dining room was open, and we were down a room service guy. Which, fortunately, didn't affect us much because most of the guests were at the dinner. They've got about half of the hotel."

"Do they do a lot of events here?"

"Not a lot, but big ones. About twice a year. The holiday party and the summer retreat."

"Did you know Mrs. Vashon?"

"Not well. Enough to bow to on the way by, if you know what I mean."

"I guess the Vashons get VIP treatment."

"*All* our guests get VIP treatment." He scanned the tables. "Excuse me for a minute."

I watched him do a circuit of the room, smiling, chatting. He knew at least one couple by name. He glided back behind the bar, made about half a dozen drinks, and delivered them. He hadn't written anything down. When he came back, he poured two orange juices, one for me and one for him.

I realized I had been mentally comparing Tom to Josh as I watched him work. Josh bitched if he had to do anything he considered menial.

"You don't mind filling in as bartender?" I asked.

Tom laughed. "I actually enjoy it. No stress, no real numbers. Brings me back to my beach bar days when it was party all night, sleep with a pretty girl, wake up, and do it all over again."

"My boss acts like it would kill him to pick up a prop and carry it to the other side of the room."

He nodded. "I know the type. That just doesn't fly here. No one says, 'that's not my job' because everything is everybody's job. Well, there's really only one job. Take care of the guest. So, whether you're in housekeeping or the hotel manager, if something needs to be done, you take care of it or make sure it's taken care of."

"Is that hard?"

"No, because everybody is on board with it. You pitch in because you know that if you need help, someone will help you."

I thought back to what Vitor said about the VashTech execs not trusting each other.

"One big happy family?"

He scoffed. "Oh, there are little squabbles now and then. Sometimes people get a little rock crazy."

"Rock crazy?"

"You're basically stuck on an island. Some days you just need to get off the island. See different people. Do something different. Summertime, we're usually too busy to even think about it. The winters are a bit slower."

"More time to think."

"More grey. Shorter days. Even here."

I nodded. Florida might be the Sunshine State, but even I counted the days to the Winter Solstice, hating that the daylight hours were shorter.

He scanned the room again, but everyone seemed content. He checked his watch.

"How long did Deputy Fletcher talk to you?"

"Travis? About two minutes of questions, then we shot the sh--breeze for a few more. We've known each other for a while."

"He seems to be taking longer with Vitor."

Tom looked uncomfortable. "Yeah."

"Did you know Vitor and Mrs. Vashon dated?"

"Yes. A few of us knew. Mr. Vashon recommended him for the job here."

I thought about how well Trip had managed Deputy Fletcher last night. "Vitor got managed."

"Sort of. I don't think he minded. Mr. Vashon basically arranged a soft landing for him."

"Got him away from Mrs. Vashon."

"Wasn't necessary on Vitor's side. I would not speculate on Mr. Vashon's motives."

"Understood." I looked at my phone. Vitor had been gone for half an hour. And I still had half a dozen props to find. "I better settle up."

"On the house," Tom said smoothly.

"Thank you." I took out another five-dollar bill. "Put it in the kitty."

He smiled. "Swing by the front desk in about half an hour and I'll make sure you have your chain."

"Thanks. Don't suppose you know where I can find a rubber chicken?"

He burst out laughing. "Maybe check the lost and found? That might be the one request we can't fulfill."

"I knew that would be a tough one. Will you be there tonight?"

"Wouldn't miss it."

I smiled innocently. He didn't know it, but he was going to be one of the ghosts tonight. Maybe even Scrooge.

I headed off to the staff dining room to see if I could get a large salad fork and some tongs. We used an oversized salad fork in the show—the kind that people hung on their walls as what passed for décor in the 1960s—but at this point, any semi-large fork would do. Tongs would be easy. The lady behind the buffet line was happy to help out.

We also needed a bell, the kind you hit on top. The gift shop had little souvenir hand bells, but they didn't have the right kind of ding, which sounds stupid, I know. They were also $16.99. I supposed I could return it after the show. Or give it as a gift to someone I wasn't overly fond of. I decided to hold off on the purchase and opted for another pack of Lorna Doones.

The clerk watched me juggle the shaker, tongs, and fork as she rang me up. She smiled. "I bet you'd like a big bag."

"Thank you!" I really wasn't thinking when I left my room."

"The curly-haired guy was already in here."

"I don't suppose he bought a bell?"

"No. But he looked at them. I thought it was kind of cute. Usually, only women look at the bells. I figured maybe his mom collected them or something."

"We're collecting props for the show tonight. We need one of those bells you hit on the top." I made a banging motion with the flat of my hand.

"Front desk. They have one."

"How did I miss that?"

"It only comes out for the midnight shift. From 6:00 am until 1:00 am, there's always someone at the front desk."

"It's not staffed after 1:00?"

"It is, but sometimes the night clerk needs to leave the desk."

"Makes sense. Thanks!"

She held open the bag and I put the props in it. We put the cookies on top so they wouldn't get crushed.

I headed over to the front desk and the clerk greeted me immediately.

"Hi, um, Tom, the Food and Beverage manager was going to leave a chain for me?" I hit the uptick at the end because it was probably a weird thing to pick up at the front desk. The clerk took it in stride.

"Oh, you're with the show. I've got it right here." He held up a two-foot length of chain.

"Perfect, thank you. I was wondering if we could also borrow the bell that the night clerk uses? We'll return everything right after the show."

That brought a big smile. "I'm pretty sure the night clerk won't mind if you *don't* bring that back. Very few people hit the bell just once." He lifted a bell from behind the counter.

"Man, you're a lifesaver. Or a show-saver."

"Happy to help. And Tom said you might want to take a look in the lost and found. Come on over here." He indicated a door to the side of the counter. I walked over to it and it opened a second later. The clerk held a large plastic tub. "Oops. Just need you to take off the lid. Sorry."

I lifted the lid. Sitting on top of a collection of hats, t-shirts, sunglasses, and various other items, was a rubber chicken.

"No!"

The clerk was laughing. "Yes."

"I cannot believe you found a rubber chicken."

He said in a formal voice, "We are a full-service facility, here to meet your every need."

"Above and beyond, for sure. Thank you so much."

"Actually, the Events Coordinator had one. Some of the groups do scavenger hunts. I don't suppose you need a huge pair of granny panties?" He pulled out a pair that would have fit a baby elephant.

"Oh, my God! Thankfully, no." He had me laughing.

"They're pretty scary. We're all looking forward to the show tonight." He set the box on a chair and put the lid back on it.

"Who's going to be running the hotel?" I asked.

"Senior staff is stepping in."

"That's really nice."

"They're good to us here. They know it's kind of isolated and they really go all out to make sure we don't go stir crazy."

"Thanks again. I'll see you a bit later."

I headed back to my room with my prizes. The red message light was blinking on my phone again. The first message was from Colin. "Let me know when you get back. I got most of the stuff. Couldn't find the right bell but we might be able to substitute a different one."

The second message was Laura. "Kasey, let me know when you're all back and I guess we'll see what we're still missing. Josh says you might need to do some quick re-writes."

No kidding.

I called Colin and told him to collect Herbie and Dan along the way. Then I flipped the latch on the door. I held off calling Laura because I hoped someone had turned up more than props. I took my Lorna Doones out of the bag and tossed them in the nightstand drawer. I could hear the guys coming down the hall. They let themselves in without knocking. Herbie was helping Dan carry things. Colin, of course, had a bag.

"Where'd you get the bag?" Dan asked, dropping his armload on the second bed. Herbie added his to the pile.

"Gift shop?"

"I wish I had thought of that."

Colin just looked at me and shook his head. Dan hadn't reached the age where you looked for easier ways to do things. Of course, I might have been juggling items in my arms if the clerk hadn't offered the bigger bag.

"Let's see what we got." Colin and I started adding what we found. We arranged them as we went along. I pulled out the rubber chicken last.

"Ta-da!"

"Oh, my God! I can't believe you found a rubber chicken," Dan said. "I was too embarrassed to even ask."

"Where did you find it?" Colin asked.

"The Food and Beverage guy tracked it down." I was lifting things from Dan's pile, spreading them out so we could see what we still needed. I lifted up a handkerchief. Underneath it was a large, plastic icicle. I slowly held it up.

"Where did you get this?"

"Off one of the Christmas trees. Half the Christmas trees in this place have them."

"Uh, Dan?" Colin started.

"Yeah, I know. We were going to cut the icicle joke, but then I saw it and grabbed it just in case."

Colin looked at me. "The deputy must have noticed..."

"We didn't. We just kind of saw decorated trees and didn't really look closely."

"So, maybe it wasn't our icicle," Colin said.

Light dawned on Dan's head. "Aw, Jeez!"

"Let's think here." I turned around slowly. "Someone killed Marie Janeé with an icicle ornament. We all thought it was the one from our prop trunk."

"Which means the killer would have had to know the icicle was in the trunk and gotten it before hand," Herbie said.

"But if it's not the prop icicle..." I handed it to Colin. "Does this feel heavier than our icicle?"

He hefted it. "A bit. Sturdier. The color is a little different, too."

"What do you think it means?" Dan asked.

"Well, for one, the hotel doesn't buy their Christmas ornaments at the dollar store."

"I guess we should make sure the deputy knows about this," Colin said.

"I'll take it down to him. In a bit."

"So, we're still cutting the joke?" Dan asked. "I mean, it's a show for the employees. We can grab another icicle. They're everywhere."

"The employees know about the icicle," Herbie said. "I mean, they know she was stabbed with an icicle."

"I guess that would be hard to keep a secret," Colin said.

"Ray, the security guy, told one of his buddies, who told a couple of people." Herbie shrugged.

"Did you find out anything else?"

"There's no coroner, but the EMTs took her body back to the fire station. The fire station and police station are all one building. Apparently, there's a..." Herbie faltered. "Like a refrigerated area for bodies? Not a real morgue, but like, I don't know. An area."

"I guess with people coming and going, boats in the summer, they probably have more than a few accidents. I mean, it's a private island, but they still need basic services." The guys nodded.

There was a knock on the door. I looked through the peephole. Laura and Josh. My room was already too people-y. I swallowed a sigh and swung the door open.

Josh immediately took charge. "Good, you're all here." He glanced over at the props. "Herbie, you're all set up and ready to go?"

"Yes, boss."

If Josh caught the snark, he ignored it. I'm pretty sure he didn't catch it; nobody expected snark from Herbie. I winked at him.

"Laura, do we have everything?"

Laura had been looking at the items and checking them off her list. "You guys did a good job. We have just about everything. Where did you find a rubber chicken?"

We laughed. "It's a full-service facility," I said.

"We weren't sure if we would need this." Colin held up the icicle.

Laura went white and made a retching noise. *Do NOT puke in my room, please God.* She held it together.

Josh snatched it out of his hand. "We will definitely not need this. Kasey, you need to cut that joke."

"Already done."

"We need to go over the script to see what else needs to be cut."

"Already checked that, too," I lied. I was not up for one-on-one face time with Josh. "We are good to go."

He harumphed. Obviously didn't get enough bossing around in. "Call is thirty minutes before the show. Herbie, I'm going to need you to help Laura carry down and set up the props. We can't put them out too early; too many people are coming and going from that room. You'll need something to carry them in."

"Under control." Dan held up a bag. "We're not idiots."

"Don't be late," Josh snapped. He tossed the icicle back on the bed and headed for the door. Laura followed in his wake.

I closed the door behind them. His cologne lingered in the room.

Dan and Herbie were bagging up the props.

"Poor Laura," I said. I meant it as in 'Poor Laura' for thinking Josh was a catch.

Dan didn't even look up. "Yeah, I thought for sure she was gonna blow chunks when she saw the icicle."

"She's been puking all weekend," Herbie said. "I don't think she's recovered from the boat ride over."

"And she's probably not looking forward to the ride back," Colin chuckled. "Didn't take her for such a puker."

I had an intuitive flash. Every so often things connected in my brain. *Poor Laura, indeed.* I kept it to myself.

"Anybody else find out anything?"

"Well, I didn't find out anything, but about half a dozen of the execs were meeting in the conference room," Colin started. "Stephen Vashon was not among them."

"Let me guess: Edward and Trip were two of them."

"Yep.

"Planning to kick him while he's down?"

"Maybe. Maybe they're just concerned about him and they are figuring out how to handle things while he's going through this."

"That's a nice thought."

"Well, I overheard one of them say 'Stephen's going to need some help' and then the door closed again. So, maybe not a corporate takeover."

I looked at Dan. "Bump into any of your lady-fans?"

"As a matter of fact, yes."

"And?"

"Not much. She was kind of sad about Marie Janeé. Well, really," he was thinking back, "she was concerned about Stephen. Said something about him being all alone at Christmas. I asked if Mr. Vashon had kids. He has two, but they don't really talk. Blame him for dumping their mother."

"Is their mother the first or second wife?"

"First, I think. They're older. Don't even live in Florida."

"That probably puts any kids in the clear," Colin said.

"I asked her if they were going to invite Stephen for Christmas so he wouldn't be alone. She looked at me like I had two heads." Dan looked confused. "I mean, if you really cared about someone and knew they were going through a hard time, wouldn't you invite them over?"

Colin said slowly, "Maybe she really wasn't all that concerned about Stephen."

"Just being polite?" Herbie asked.

"Maybe." Colin shrugged.

"Vitor said something interesting to me. He said the VashTech people pretty much all liked each other but they didn't trust each other. So, maybe the relationships don't go very deep."

"Sad," Dan observed.

We were silent, soaking that in.

"Well, at least we have us!" Herbie broke the silence.

"Amen."

I looked around. "We've got about an hour and a half. I'm going to run down and just check with Deputy Fletcher about the icicle. He'll probably think I'm meddling again."

"Do you want me to go with you?" Colin asked.

"No, I'm good. Thanks."

The guys picked up the props and scooted out the door. The icicle was left on the bed. I picked it up, put my keycard in my back pocket, and headed downstairs.

Alcoholism as an Alibi? Why Not?

If Deputy Fletcher thought I was meddling, he kept it to himself. I produced the icicle and told him that they were on every tree. Maybe the icicle that was used to kill Marie Janeé didn't come from our props trunk.

"It didn't. It was an icicle from one of the resort trees. Your prop icicle was in the pile of props. And," he paused. "Two different makes of icicle."

"We noticed the resort's icicle has more heft."

"How did you come up with this one?" he asked.

"We're going to do the show tonight for the employees and we needed props. Since you're holding ours as evidence."

"Sorry about that. You'll most likely get them back in a few days. Once we find out who did this."

I wanted to ask how it was going, but he wasn't going to tell me one way or the other. Better to nibble from the sides.

"There must be a reason Marie Janeé was killed, not someone else," I ventured.

"There's always a reason; sometimes it's not a good reason."

"But this isn't random."

"No. And the most likely suspects all have solid alibis."

"Including Vitor?"

He nodded. I breathed a sigh of relief. I liked him and more than that, didn't want to think my instincts were so far off that I'd chatted up a killer without feeling some suspicion.

"When do you think the storm will clear?"

"Sometime in the night."

"Well, you'll get some backup in the morning."

"Yes, but whoever did this can make their way off the island if they have access to a boat. And frankly, there are about forty of them sitting down at the pier, any one of which can make the trip across."

"You need to find out who did this before the storm dies."

He nodded. "I've got about fifteen hours to figure this out or my ass is grass."

"Well, it's not as if you had the resources to handle this. You're out here on your own in the middle of a storm."

"Yeah, well, that's kind of my fault, too. My buddy had a hot date in Bonita Springs. He was supposed to be my backup and I told him to take the night off. He should have been back this morning, but of course, he can't get across. He's going to get into trouble, too, which makes me feel worse."

"If you can solve this murder, no one will say boo."

"Oh, they'll still say boo, but we'll keep our jobs. I need to pull this one off." He sighed. In response to my questioning look he said, "So far, nothing. I'm plodding through, checking all the boxes."

It was time to come clean. "My friends and I are kind of hanging out, talking to some of the VashTech people."

"I'm not going to even bother telling you to keep out of it. Anything you turn up, I appreciate."

My eyes slid off to the side. He caught it.

"It doesn't mean you have my permission. I'm just pretending not to know what you're doing."

"Deniability?"

"Total."

"Anything we should be listening for?"

"There is a major gap in the timeline."

I shifted forward in my chair.

"Marie Janeé was last seen in the ladies' room near the lobby. Right near your Green Room and the event room, but across the hall and down." He waited. I caught up.

"How or why did she end up in the Green Room?"

"Exactly. How does she get from the ladies' room into the Green Room?"

"So, you've established she was killed there."

"Yes."

It made sense. There had been a lot of blood, mostly in the props trunk, but some on the carpet, too.

"Would blood have... sprayed on the killer?"

"Absolutely. We have spray droplets that go out twelve feet. She was killed near the tree in the Green Room—"

"So, you knew from the start that the icicle wasn't from our show."

"Yes."

We had been really slow on that. Then again, we had been in shock and not really taking in the whole scene. Fletcher had had time to go through everything.

"So, I send her into the ladies' room. Irene sees her in there and leaves. Or said she did."

"Irene Winship Yes. And, since she didn't walk into dinner with blood on her dress, she's in the clear."

"Unless she had some sort of covering, but that would involve preparation. And frankly, she was a little too in-the-bag to pull it off."

He nodded. "Alcoholism as an alibi."

"Can I look at your timeline?"

"You might as well." He rubbed his hands over his face as I came around to his side of his work table.

I read through his notes. His handwriting was neat, concise. A bit like a draftsman.

"I don't suppose you want to confess?"

"Still a no. Though," I said, my finger tracing down his notes, "I can see why you keep asking. I was on the scene."

"And you went up and changed."

I gave him a look.

"I know. Don't worry. You're in the clear. I'm just tired. Do you remember anything else? Walk me through it."

I thought back. "I left Marie Janeé at the ladies' room, saw Laura who was looking for Josh. I went into the elevator..." I stopped.

"What?"

"I heard Laura say, 'There you are' so Josh must have been just a little bit behind me."

"Yes. They said they went into dinner and didn't see Marie Janeé."

"Okay. So, somewhere between the ladies' room and the Green Room, Marie Janeé met up with someone, went into the Green Room..."

"Or was forced into the Green Room."

"Or forced. She was very petite. It wouldn't be hard for most anyone to grab her."

He nodded.

"Perhaps they argue. Perhaps the killer immediately stabs her."

"They most likely argued. If you were going to kill someone, you'd bring a weapon. A plastic icicle would not be someone's first choice as a murder weapon."

"So, anger. Maybe even passion."

"Marie Janeé could have been having an affair with someone else, maybe someone in the company."

I shook my head. "I doubt it. Stephen is the CEO. She already had the alpha male in the group. She had found her meal ticket. I don't think she would do anything to screw the marriage up."

"So maybe, it was someone who wanted Marie Janeé sexually. She turned him down."

I remembered her kneeing Josh. "She was very good at shutting down advances."

"So, we look at the men."

"Or, maybe one of the wives thought Marie Janeé was too interested in her husband. Whether she was or not. Could a woman have stabbed her?"

"Possible, but not likely. Statistically, only about fourteen percent of murderers are women."

"This was a crime of opportunity. Not premeditated."

"Which rules out the husband. If he had hired someone, the killer would have brought a weapon."

It was my turn to nod. "Too many suspects. Too little time."

"I have at least fifty suspects at this point."

"That's not counting the hotel workers."

"Or any of the hotel workers," he agreed. "Narrowing this down is a nightmare."

I had an idea. "We're doing a show for the employees at five. We were going to cut the bit with the icicle out of the show. What if we keep it in and you can see if anyone reacts? I mean, the killer might not be an employee or even be at the show, but if someone does react..." I trailed off. "Kind of grasping at straws, aren't I?"

"Frankly, straws are all I have at this point. Keep it in. In the meantime, if you think of anything, let me know."

"Will do."

I picked up the icicle and went back up to my room. I had an hour and a half before I had to be down in the staff dining room for the show. I needed some time to think.

I DO MY BEST thinking chewing on Twizzlers. At least that's what I tell myself. Mostly I just like Twizzlers. I pulled out a pad of paper and a pen and sat down at the little table. Start at the beginning. What do we know so far?

1) I saw Marie Janeé go into the ladies' room.

2) Irene said she saw Marie Janeé in the ladies' room and left immediately.

3) I heard Laura say "There you are" to Josh.

I scratched out the "to Josh." I heard her say the words; I was assuming it was Josh.

4) I got on the elevator, went back to the room, changed, and went down to the dining room. Colin, Dan, and Herbie were already there. Colin and Dan had changed; Herbie was still in his show clothes. No blood on any of them.

5) At some point, Marie Janeé went into or was forced into the Green Room where she was murdered and stuffed in the props trunk.

6) Josh left the dinner to tell us to find Marie Janeé.

I circled item five. That was the big hole that needed filling. We didn't really even know how much time was involved. Maybe forty-five minutes to an hour? Maybe less. I had no way of knowing.

I decided to try another direction. Who had opportunity and motive? I realized I didn't know enough about Marie Janeé to figure out who had a motive to kill her. Or even the opportunity. We needed to know who wasn't in the banquet room or who came in late. I made a note to ask Deputy Fletcher if anyone had taken pictures during the dinner. There would be an electronic time stamp on them. Of course, the murderer could have been at the dinner, gone out for a few minutes and come back in. But then they would have some sort of blood spatter on them, so no. If they were in the banquet room, odds were very good that they weren't the killer.

I threw the pen down and it bounced across the table. All my speculation was useless. We just didn't have enough verifiable information.

There was a knock on my door. I looked through the peephole and opened the door to let Josh in, hoping that my face wasn't registering the dismay I felt.

"News?" I asked, hoping to bring him right to the point. He sat at the little table and immediately started reading my notes. I crossed the room and snatched them up, but not quickly enough.

"You missed the part where I may have screwed up," he said. "I need your help."

Josh admitting a mistake? Both my eyebrows shot up at this. Josh never admits making a mistake.

"Not locking the Green Room door?"

"Worse." He slumped in the chair.

"You came here to tell me, so tell me."

"You're a girl, right?"

"Last time I checked."

"I mean, you would have some, I don't know... insight." He sighed. "I think I really screwed things up with Laura."

"No shit, Sherlock. She totally caught the lipstick on your collar."

"Worse than that."

"Not sure what could be worse than getting caught hitting on an old girlfriend."

"I may have said the wrong thing about her dress for the dinner."

"Really? Your ex-girlfriend gets murdered minutes after she shoots you down and your big screwup was not admiring your girlfriend's dress? In the grand scheme of things, Josh, that's pretty minor."

"Well, I get that." His sarcasm was knee-deep. I stared him down. "But Laura is mad at me. She won't even look at me, and every time I turn around, she's puking. She says I make her sick."

I had my own thoughts on what was making her sick. I was also very sure I was not the one to break the happy news to him. I sat in the other chair.

"What did you say to her?"

"I was pissed off that Marie Janeé had shot me down, so I just wasn't in the mood. And Laura was on me for being late for the dinner, even though we weren't—people were still going in. Anyway, I said she looked like a cheap imitation of Marie Janeé in that dress." He mumbled the last part.

"You said WHAT?"

"I might have said she looked like a dollar store version of Marie Janeé. I mean, they both have blond hair and it was a red dress kind of like Marie Janeé's and I just was…"

"Being an asshole."

To his credit, he didn't fight my assessment.

"So, then what happened?"

"She said she had brought another dress and was going to change into that. I told her I'd meet her in the banquet room."

I thought back to last night. I hadn't even noticed that Laura had changed dresses. I felt dizzy. Could Laura have killed Marie Janeé? If Laura had killed Josh, that would be understandable. Would she have been jealous enough to kill Marie Janeé? It would have taken her some time to clean up afterwards.

"How long did she take to change?" I asked.

"I don't know. Fifteen, twenty minutes? The usual time. I was talking to some of the executives. There were more pre-dinner cocktails. We didn't all go in and immediately sit down."

"How did she seem? Was she upset?"

"Obviously, she was upset with me. But really, she should have been a little bit thankful that I was saving her from unfavorable comparisons."

I tried to wrap my brain around his justification for being so nasty to Laura. My brain came back with a big, fat *Nope, not gonna ever understand that one.* If Laura didn't kill Josh for saying that, she had even less motive for killing Marie Janeé. If he had said that to me, he'd be walking funny for a week.

I tried a different tact. "Did you notice anyone else who came in late?"

"Not really. I was trying to line up some funding for the company. People had just seen the show, they enjoyed it. I figured I'd strike while the iron was hot."

Hitting people up for money in the middle of a corporate party. Josh was all class.

"Does the troupe need money? I thought the shows paid for themselves and then some."

"I'm working on getting us our own venue to put on shows so we don't have to pay for the hall or the caterers. Most of the money we charge for the dinner shows goes straight to the venue. If I have my own place, I can cut our costs."

I nodded. It made sense from a business standpoint. But his timing was lousy. I looked at the room clock. I needed to start getting ready soon. "What do you want me to do?"

"Could you talk to Laura and tell her that Marie Janeé made the pass at me?"

"That ship has already sailed, Josh. It's all on you to make it up to her."

"What should I do?"

"How about starting with treating her better? And not just for a few days, but from now on. You treat her like a personal assistant, not your girlfriend. Compliment her. Tell her she looks nice. Take her out on a real date instead of making every dinner out about business so you can write it off." Laura had let a few things slip to me over the months we'd worked together. She might be too timid to bring them up to Josh, but I wasn't.

"I treat her well!"

"You don't treat anyone well. Read the room, Josh. People don't like you. Most people who know you wouldn't spit on you if you were on fire. Maybe you should try being nicer to people in general and Laura in particular."

"I'm not trying to make friends; I'm running a business."

"You don't need to make friends. You do need people to like you if you want them to help you build your business. If you don't treat people well, they won't stay very long. Doesn't matter if they're employees or girlfriends. You need to take a good hard look in the mirror or you're going to be very alone for the rest of your life."

"Well, I came here for help, not criticism." He stood up with a huff. It could have been indignation, but I knew I had hit a nerve.

"No, you came here for me to tell you that what you said to Laura was not so bad. It was bad, Josh and it was particularly stupid to say it when you had Marie Janeé's lipstick all over you. So, no. I'm not the bad guy here. Laura's not the bad guy. You know what you did was wrong. You said it when you walked through the door. So go back, apologize to her, and hope that she doesn't dump your ass because she is your human credibility."

"She's my what?"

"Your human credibility. People like her. They do things for her, not for you. If you can't treat people well, you need to have someone close to you who can. Laura functions as a buffer zone for you. You lose her, you're going to lose half your actors."

He paled. "I was running this company before Laura ever showed up."

"And I'm willing to bet you were constantly replacing actors."

"So what? Actors are a dime a dozen."

"Tampa is a small town and people in theatre here all know each other. Your reputation is not great. You pay well, but you have to—people don't want to work with you. Sure, there are always new people coming up who want to break into show business. And you take advantage of that. But it's inefficient. You're constantly having to call rehearsals to bring the new people up to speed. Unpaid rehearsals. Which pisses off the people you already have. So, they leave. You have to spend time auditioning people. You need to resize costumes or buy new ones."

"Well, when I need a business consultant, I'll hire one. I've done pretty well so far. And, may I remind you that you work for me."

"And that can change. May I remind you that you came to me for advice. I gave it. If you want someone to suck up to you, well, you're going to have to hold auditions again."

I moved to the door and held it open. "I need to get ready for call."

He swept out, his face red with anger and I hoped at least a little embarrassment. I sighed as I closed the door. I was most likely out of acting work after tonight's show. I had wanted to get experience and I certainly got that. I made a mental note to check out other theatre troupes in the area and then took my costume out of the closet. Time to make like an elf.

Singing for Our Supper

As expected, Laura and Herbie were busy setting up for the show. They were usually the first ones to arrive and the last to leave. There was a small area screened off as a "backstage" which just barely had room enough to stow our stuff. The staff dining room was closed off for the half hour before the show so we could move around and set up. We could hear people working in the kitchen and from time to time, someone would come out and stock silverware or glasses.

I had recommended Tom, the F&B Manager to be our Scrooge, a step up from one of the ghosts. We had originally talked about having the hotel manager do it, but he was still shaken up and dealing with Marie Janeé's murder. Tom was easy-going with a good sense of humor. He was also high enough up in the management chain that the employees would enjoy seeing him doing goofy things. He came in from the back kitchen and we ran him through the pre-show drill.

"Did you get the rubber chicken?"

"I can't believe you had one!" I said. "You saved the show. And being Scrooge is your reward."

"I'm not sure it's a reward," he ventured.

"They're gonna love you."

He smiled. "Well, yeah. Of course."

"Laura has your lines on cue cards." I looked around the room. It was not an ideal set up for Laura. She'd have to kind of kneel on the floor so she wouldn't be blocking people's views. "Can we get some kind of cushion or at least a towel for Laura?"

Herbie saw the problem immediately and hustled off to find something.

Colin, Dan, and I hung around the screened area.

"Tom is a good choice," Dan said. "He actually has timing."

"Yeah. I talked with him in the bar earlier. He's fun."

"We should use the gift shop lady for one of the ghosts," Colin said. "She was really helpful."

"Okay. Colin, you pick her out for Christmas Past."

"I'm picking out one of the buffet line workers for one of the ghosts. They've been really nice," Dan said.

Colin and I nodded. Outside of Scrooge, we pretty much chose people randomly.

With that set, I said, "We're leaving the icicle bit in."

"Really?" Colin physically drew back.

"Yeah. Deputy Fletcher wants to watch the employees, to see if any of them react to seeing it."

"What did Josh say?"

"I didn't tell him. Or Laura."

They looked at me, puzzled.

"I didn't want to argue with them. You know how Josh likes to control every last bit. The deputy wants it; I'll do it."

I had my own reasons for not telling Josh and Laura. I waited until Laura did her final check of the props and then pre-set the icicle in its normal spot, just to the side of the "stage" area.

"Doors are about to open, people," Josh said. "Places."

Places meant that Dan, Colin, and I were stuck behind the screen for the next ten minutes or so. Close quarters.

"So, we're not changing any of the lines?" Dan asked.

"Nope. We run it as is."

They nodded. We leaned against the wall, waiting.

"The glamor of show business," Colin commented.

"We are literally singing for our supper." Dan laughed. "It will make a good story when I'm being interviewed on *The Tonight Show*."

"Remember us when you make it big," I said.

Josh blew into the microphone then ran through the introduction. The music started and we bounded out, full of happy-happy and merry-merry. We got a big laugh when we chose Tom to be Scrooge and he mugged shamelessly when he put on the substitute Santa hat. I saw Vitor in the crowd and mentally elected not to use him as a ghost. I wanted to watch him during the icicle bit. I recognized a few people in the audience; I figured Colin and Dan did, too. We would have enough people to choose from.

Colin pulled up the gift shop clerk for Christmas Past. She was nervous so I whispered, "This is your punishment for helping us." She laughed and relaxed a bit. I chose the desk clerk for Christmas Present. With each person we chose to bring up, there were hoots and comments. Murder or not, the employees were ready to have a good time.

Hotel people, like waiters and really, anyone who deals with the public, are pretty good at playing along. The employees were delighted to see their coworkers get hauled up on stage. Deputy Fletcher was leaning against the wall. He was in a good position to watch the audience. We were coming up on the icicle bit. I looked over and nodded at him. He didn't change his position, but his eyes started scanning.

Scrooge was having his epiphany. Colin leaned on Tom, propping his elbow on Tom's shoulder, and pulled out the icicle.

"Ehhh, what's up Scrooge?"

I saw Herbie at the sound board, looking up in surprise. Laura, kneeling in front of us, momentarily dropped the cue card with Scrooge's next line. I whispered it to Tom.

"OMG! I am like, just now realizing I'm a total jerk!" He got a nice laugh.

"No kidding," Colin came back.

"But if you sign up for my self-development course at the low, low price of $99.95, I can help you with that," Dan slid in between them, holding an oversized, spiral bound manual with the title "How to Stop Being a Total Jerk, Scrooge." For some reason, that got a bigger laugh than it usually got. Which was good. It gave Laura time to move the dropped card to the "used" stack and make sure she had the right one showing.

I had intended to watch Vitor, but I got distracted when Laura dropped the cards. I hoped Deputy Fletcher had kept his eye on the employees. We ran through the last six minutes of the show, sang the carols, and took our bows. I was glad there was no official Meet and Greet. We stood behind the screened partition and waited for the audience members to start moving around so we could come back out again with as little notice as possible. It didn't take long. People were talking and laughing. Some had to get back to work. Others hung around, waiting for the kitchen workers to start putting out the stainless-steel trays of food.

Josh came back to the screen and said, "Five minutes in the Conference Room for show notes." He was not happy. As usual.

I looked at the guys. "I'll take the rap for the icicle bit. He's going to fire me anyway."

"He can't fire you until we've done all the Christmas Carol gigs," Colin pointed out.

"Exactly. He's pissed but he's also not going to lose out on making money. Maybe he'll be over it by the time Christmas rolls around."

Laura was putting the props into a cardboard box. Herbie was packing up his equipment. Josh was making nice with Tom, who gave me a wave as we went by. I knew from experience that Josh would take at least ten minutes to get to the Conference Room. He liked to keep people waiting.

We headed over to the Business Center, jingling all the way. The three of us sat at the end of the table closest to the door. Josh eventually showed up with Laura. I assumed Herbie had been excused from the meeting. He rarely had any notes from Josh.

Josh stood at the head of the table. Laura sat on his right. She looked even paler than usual, but I had figured out the reason for that. In spite of my lecture this afternoon, or maybe because of it, Josh was in full form.

"Well, that was a total mess. What do you have to say for yourselves?"

"I thought it went fine," Colin said. "What didn't you like?"

"You forgot to take the icicle bit out, for starters. That was horrible. Just horrible."

I spoke up. "That was my fault, Josh. I meant to tell them to take it out and somehow overlooked it."

"You didn't make any of the changes you were supposed to," Josh said.

"It didn't seem to affect the show," Dan pointed out. "The employees loved it. And that manager guy seemed to be okay with things."

"That's not the point. You were told to make the changes and you didn't."

"Sorry about that, Josh. It won't happen again." I was getting good at acting sincere.

"You're not sorry. You purposely defied me. And you upset Laura."

Maybe not so good at the sincere thing. But at least he was making good with Laura. I should have known better.

"And what the hell was that, Laura? Dropping the cue card? Talk about pulling focus from the actors!"

Laura finally fought back. "I dropped one card. One. In all the shows I've done. Maybe you should try kneeling on a nasty floor for forty-five minutes!"

Josh back-peddled. "Well, if you're not physically up for this."

"There's nothing wrong with me physically! The card slipped all of what, eighteen inches? Kasey covered. It was fine."

"Don't let it happen again."

I shook my head. This was not the guy Laura wanted to have a baby with. I hoped she realized that. I mumbled, "Not my circus, not my monkeys." Colin gave me a questioning look. "Later," I mouthed.

Josh spent another five minutes telling us we were basically useless and unprofessional and we needed to schedule a rehearsal before the next show. Colin put a stop to that.

"We know the show. It was a one-off. And I don't have time to make a rehearsal. We're all busy and overscheduled right now. You want to call a rehearsal? Fine, but I can't make it."

Josh looked at us.

"My calendar is maxed out," I said.

"This is my busy season." Dan stood up, towering over all of us. "I'm booked up and most of the jobs pay better than this."

Josh recognized a mutiny when he saw one. "Well, just make sure your next show is letter perfect."

We left without waiting to be dismissed. I wondered if Laura was going to tell him exactly why she dropped the cards. We jingled our way through the lobby, where the desk clerk gave us a shout out, and got into the elevator.

Colin looked at me. "What's the deal with Laura?"

"Pale? Puking all the time? Having trouble holding her position?"

"Oh."

"Yeah."

"What?" Dan asked.

We looked at him. Colin made a curving motion over his stomach.

"She's pregnant?"

"Duh."

"Josh shouldn't pick on her like that! That's so wrong, man."

"Josh hasn't figured it out yet."

Dan looked at me. "He really shouldn't be a dad. You have to have patience with little kids. And, you know, actually be a decent human being."

The elevator doors opened and we headed down to our rooms.

"See you guys in the staff dining room!" Colin said.

"I might be a little late. Start without me." I put the keycard in the slot. I wanted to check notes with Deputy Fletcher.

***

I was a little more careful removing my elf makeup this time around. I opened the door to leave and Laura was standing there.

"Hey, you need something?"

"Yes. No." She looked like she was about to turn around. "Yes."

"Come on in."

She sat in one of the club chairs at the table. I sat on the bed.

"Thanks for sticking up for me."

"Josh was out of line. As usual." I paused. "What are you going to do?"

"About what?"

"About the baby."

"Oh, God. How do you know?"

"Four years of college with panicked girlfriends?" I reached for her hand. "The question is, have you told Josh?"

"I just did."

"And?"

She started crying. "He said, 'I suppose I'll have to marry you.' He sounded like the whole thing was so... so... *distasteful* to him. You know that voice."

I did. I could not believe he said that. Then again, I could. If he had been in front of me, I would have throttled him with my bare hands. Instead, I grabbed the box of tissues from the nightstand.

"Listen, Laura, you don't have to have this baby. And you certainly don't have to put up with Josh even if you do decide to have the baby." Inside I was thinking: *These are not genetics that should be passed on.* I'm proud to say I kept that part to myself.

She nodded. "I don't know what I'm going to do. But this weekend with Josh has shown me that I don't want to be with him. Or have my child exposed to him for that matter."

Good call.

"Don't say anything to the others about this, okay? I just have to get through this weekend, get off this stupid island, and figure it out from there."

"Mum's the word on splitting with Josh, but we had already figured out you were pregnant."

"The guys know?"

"Yes. Well, maybe Herbie doesn't, but he's having dinner with Dan and Colin so I'm pretty sure he'll know in the next half hour."

She blushed. "Oh, God. I'm so embarrassed."

"Why? You did nothing wrong. Josh is the one who should be embarrassed. I mean, if we figured it out and he didn't... let's just say he doesn't deserve to be a dad."

She smiled at me and blew her nose.

"Do you want to have dinner with us in the staff dining room?" I asked.

"Yes, but I can't. I have to do the dinner with the corporate bigwigs. Which is my other reason for coming here. Do you have a dress I can borrow? I wore the burgundy one last night and I can't even look at the red dress that Josh and Marie Janeé made fun of."

"Marie Janeé made fun of your dress, too? Was she there?"

"I ran into her outside the Green Room. She was coming down the hall and heard what Josh said."

"And?"

Laura started tearing up again. "She looked at the dress I was going to change into and said 'I used to have to shop the discount stores.' I thought she was going to be nice, but no. She said Josh was right; I looked like a wannabe. Then she told me that I was so pathetic that I couldn't even keep Josh interested in me. 'You might want to keep Josh on a tighter leash, sweetie.' That's exactly what she said. That's when I knew the lipstick was hers."

I nodded. There had been no need for Marie Janeé to rub it in. Bad enough Laura was dating Josh. What was wrong with people? They made it up to the next rung and instead of helping someone else up, they wanted to pretend they had never been one of the 'lesser' people. It wasn't only comics and actors who were insecure. Seemed like everybody was keeping track of what the next person had.

I went over to my closet and pulled out the dress I had brought for the Meet and Greet. It was a jade green sleeveless cocktail shift. Not fancy, but it had a little bit of detail on it.

"This might be a bit long on you, but not too bad," I said. I reached back into the closet and pulled out the black, long-sleeved, cropped jacket that I had brought to wear over it.

"Thanks so much."

"Tell Josh I said he's an asshole."

"I take it you won't be working for him after this show?"

"I'm pretty sure I'll be fired."

"Well, I'm the company manager as well as stage manager." She smiled at me. "I have a say in who gets fired. Or not."

"Thanks for that. But I'm good with leaving the troupe."

She sighed. "I might be right behind you."

I watched her walk down the hall. I should have offered to share my room tonight but there was an off chance she had murdered Marie Janeé. I was ninety-nine percent sure she hadn't, but the one percent was not a chance I wanted to take. I checked my back pocket to make sure I had my keycard, waited until I saw her door close, then headed down to the elevators to find Deputy Fletcher.

Deputy Fletcher was not in the event room. I looked around the lobby but didn't see him. He could have been anywhere, including going home to change. I looked out at the rain and hoped he kept a go-bag in his cruiser. It was still too nasty out there to drive, even short distances.

When in doubt, eat. I headed over to the staff dining room. Colin, Dan, and Herbie were already half-way through their meals. I went through the line, got all the best comfort foods: shepherd's pie, mac n'cheese, and a big piece of chocolate cake. I wasn't ready to fill the guys in on my latest bit of information. I hoped I was wrong about Laura.

"What kept you?" Colin asked, moving a few plates to give me room.

"Laura came to borrow a dress for tonight."

"Did you talk about, you know...?" Colin asked.

"She told Josh she's pregnant, so I guess we can say that out loud now."

Herbie looked up from his mashed potatoes. "How did Josh take it?"

"With his usual lack of grace."

"Are they going to get married?" Dan asked.

"Well, as marriage proposals go—"

"He proposed?" Herbie cut in, his eyes wide.

"The worst marriage proposal in the world. He said, and I quote, 'Well I guess this means I'm supposed to marry you' unquote."

"Even I'm not that much of an idiot," Colin said.

"He really said that?" Dan asked.

"Yep. Worse, she's considering it."

"Why in the world would she even?"

"They're living together. Finances are probably mixed. The idea that a kid should have both parents if possible. I mean, having a kid on your own is expensive as hell. Choosing to be a single mother is not an easy path."

"She could, you know..." Dan said.

"Have an abortion. Yeah. Which means that the fewer people who know she's pregnant, the better it will be for her. She probably doesn't want us discussing something that private."

Herbie said quietly, "She'd make a good mom. She's always keeping us in line."

We agreed.

"Just a shame it's going to have Josh's genes," Colin said.

"My thoughts exactly." I gave a little shudder of repulsion.

"So, do we all pretend we don't know?" Dan asked.

"Probably best for now. Let her announce it. Or not." I didn't want to think about the added complication of perhaps having that baby in prison. I wanted to talk over the situation with Deputy Fletcher and get his thoughts. At this point, Laura was the last person to have seen Marie Janeé alive. I was hoping there was something I missed that would prove Laura didn't kill her.

"A lot of changes coming up for our little troupe," Colin said.

"How so?" Herbie asked.

"Well, we're probably all going to get fired, with the exception of you, for starters," Dan answered.

"I'm leaving after these shows are done." The statement just came flying out of my mouth. Did I mention I'm a blurter?

"No, don't go!" Dan said.

"You make it fun. And funny," Colin added.

Herbie looked at me. "You've had enough of Josh's bullshit."

I nodded. "It's not that I can't take it. It's just that I don't have to. The meeting we had tonight... Dan when you stood up and we all just left... it kind of turned on the lightbulb in my head. I could just leave. I mean, there are other acting groups in the area. We all know that."

"I like the work," Dan said. "It's fun to do the shows, but they're already on my resume. It's not like I'm actually doing any serious acting. It's all pretty campy, really."

"I do it for the fun of it," Colin said. "But Josh is making it not fun. I mean, it's fun to make fun of him..."

"That's a lot of fun," I pointed out. We all laughed, the tension broken. "What about you, Herbie?"

He looked surprised.

"Josh pretty much lets me do my own thing. He's mostly just inconsiderate."

"He'd be up the creek without you," Dan said.

"No. He'd just get another sound guy. But it's a fairly good gig for me. I'm probably going to stick around." He sighed. "I hate to think of you guys leaving."

"Josh makes a good common enemy," Colin noted and we all laughed in agreement.

I had worked my way through the meal carbs. I stacked the mac n'cheese bowl on the empty dinner plate and pushed them to the side. Time to work on the dessert carbs. I decided a cup of coffee would enhance the experience. I went to the coffee area and when I came back, the guys had moved on to getting off the island.

"I heard one of the workers say the first ferry out wouldn't be here until at least noon."

"At least we can sleep in," Dan said.

"I'm going to have to call in to work. If the phones are working. And if we don't get off here until noon, we won't get to Tampa until at least three. That's a day's pay for me." I sighed. Josh better come through with some bonus money.

"I'll send out an email to my students," Colin started. "Oh. No, I won't. Jeez, I hope we get wifi back early in the morning." Usually, Colin took everything with good humor. This was really the first time I'd seen him look upset.

"You like your students."

"Yeah, they're great kids. Of course, the kids I have in class want to learn this stuff. In my first few years, I had to teach the lower-level courses and I had a lot of kids in there who were just collecting a science credit for their degrees."

"Yeah, but is it fun for you? I mean, wouldn't you give up your day job in a minute for the glamor of show business?" I kidded him.

He laughed. But then he got serious. "I made it a goal in life to have as much fun as possible. And when it stops being fun, I stop doing it."

"Like these shows," Herbie said. He sounded a little sad.

"The shows are fun. Josh is not. So, that's a consideration. It may just be time to leave. The not fun stuff is starting to outweigh the fun stuff."

"I like working with all of you," Dan said. "It is fun. Really, Josh is the only downside."

I finished my cake. "Maybe we'll all end up working together on some other project. Plus, you have to come see me do stand-up. I never have anyone in the audience. I could use the support."

"Definitely. Let us know where you're performing."

"I'll get my students to come, too," Colin said.

I lifted my coffee cup in a toast. "Here's to better venues."

We clinked glasses.

"So, movie night in your room, Kasey?"

"No cable, remember?"

"I've got movies downloaded on my laptop," Colin said. If we have an RGB cable, I can hook it up to the TV."

"I've got several of those cables," Herbie said. "I'll bring them."

"Good to have a friend who's a techie," Dan slapped Herbie on the back.

"I have to do some stuff. Can you guys amuse yourself for an hour or so?"

"Sure. We have to get more beer and snacks, anyway."

"I think there's still a six pack in my fridge," I offered.

"As I said, we need to get more beer," Dan joked.

"Okay. You guys are in charge of food and entertainment. I'll catch up with you in an hour."

"Synchronizing watches," Dan held up his wrist, looking at a nonexistent watch. "Synchronizing cell phones?"

We laughed. I brought my plates over to the dish station and headed out. Time to find Deputy Fletcher.

Getting Crowded Under the Bus

This time, Deputy Fletcher was exactly where I expected him to be, in the event room. The door to the room was open, but I hesitated at the doorway, not sure if I should knock. He looked up and waved me in. I took the time to close the door behind me.

"You've got something." It was a statement.

I nodded. I felt like I was throwing Laura under the bus. Mostly because I was. I told him about Josh calling Laura a second-rate Marie Janeé. Fletcher sucked in his breath on that one.

"Yeah, I know. Welcome to Josh."

He made a note.

"But then Marie Janeé added insult to injury. Laura told me that she saw Marie Janeé in the hallway as she was heading to the ladies' to change her outfit."

"Marie Janeé was going out as she was going in?"

"Right outside the Green Room." I let it hang.

"Did not see that one coming," he muttered.

"It doesn't mean she killed Marie Janeé," I started.

"But it does mean she lied to me. Or omitted," he corrected himself. "Both of them did. They said they went into the dinner together. She's got motive, opportunity, and means."

"But why would she tell me that she saw Marie Janeé if she killed her? I mean, if it were me and no one knew I had seen the victim, I wouldn't tell anyone."

"She was upset. She was talking to a friend. She probably didn't think you'd put two and two together. Or more likely, she didn't think at all. People feel guilty and they blurt things out."

"There's something else."

He waited.

"Laura is pregnant."

"By Josh, I assume?"

"Yeah. And he was less than happy about the news."

"I can imagine."

I shook my head. "I know I'm biased, but I don't think Laura could kill someone."

"Because she's pregnant? That might give her more motivation to kill Marie Janeé."

"So, women get all hormonal and can't control themselves? Believe me, there'd be a lot more dead husbands and boyfriends if that were true."

"Because Marie Janeé was a threat to her relationship with Josh. At that point, Laura didn't know that Marie Janeé wasn't interested in Josh. She probably had seen the lipstick on Josh's collar and assumed the worst." Fletcher nodded slowly to himself. I could see him putting the pieces together.

"Doesn't a person's basic character have anything to do with it? Because Laura is one of the nicest people on the planet. And she's super-passive, a doormat really."

"Many people who are treated poorly reach a turning point where they decide they won't take that kind of treatment any more. Being pregnant might have been the push that made Laura start standing up for herself."

I thought of how she had pushed back in the meeting when Josh started yelling at her. I tried to wrap my head around Laura killing someone.

"You didn't check Laura and Josh's clothes. And she needed to borrow a dress from me tonight. Said she couldn't even look at the other one."

"Crap." He stood up.

"What should I do?"

"I've got it from here. And thanks."

We left the room and I saw him head to the manager's office.

I HAD THE DOOR latch flipped around in anticipation of the guys showing up, which also meant I could hear what was going on in the hall. Less than ten minutes later, I heard the manager and deputy knock on Josh's room door. It was a courtesy. Josh and Laura were at dinner and Deputy Fletcher knew it. I wondered if anyone else would notice.

A few minutes later, Colin softly knocked on my door and let himself in.

"The deputy and hotel manager are in Josh's room," he whispered to me.

"I know."

"Do they think Josh killed Marie Janeé?"

"Laura."

"Laura?" He forgot to whisper.

"Shhhh."

He ducked his head. "But that's just stupid."

"Is it?"

We heard Dan come out of his room and Herbie greeting him.

"What's happening in Josh's room?" Dan asked.

"Beats me," Herbie replied.

They crossed over to my room. Dan didn't bother knocking. I reversed the latch and closed the door tightly behind them.

"What's going on?"

"Deputy Fletcher is checking Laura's clothes for blood." I kept my voice low.

"He thinks Laura killed Marie Janeé?" Dan looked at all of us.

Herbie turned white. "She'd never do that. Laura is one of the kindest people I've ever met!"

I brought them up to speed on what Laura had told me.

"Gee. I thought Marie Janeé was kind of snotty, but what she said to Laura was just cruel. How small a person do you have to be?" Colin was disgusted.

"Well, it was petty, but I don't think she deserved to die," Dan said.

"Fletcher is thinking it was an in-the-moment thing. Which would make sense." I trailed off.

"No. Laura can't be the killer." Herbie sounded almost desperate.

"Well, she's pregnant and she might be feeling very protective..."

"No! Laura is NOT the killer." Herbie looked around, his eyes a bit wild. Then he shrank down. "I work with her all the time. It's just not in her."

Colin stepped in. "I agree. And there's no proof yet so why don't we just wait and see what the deputy turns up. I bet it's a big fat nothing-burger."

Herbie looked relieved.

"Let's go with that," I said.

"Are they still in there?" Dan asked.

We all looked at each other and then moved to the door. I looked through the peephole.

"Door is still open. Nope, wait."

"What!"

"Shhh."

"They're coming out. He's got something in his hands."

"What?"

"I can't tell. This peephole makes everything distorted. They're heading for the elevator."

I turned around. "It's probably the red dress she was wearing before she changed."

We were silent. We slowly went back to our usual seats.

"I need a drink," Dan said.

"Don't we all," Colin agreed.

Beers were handed around. I offered up the scotch. I thought the situation called for something stronger, but there were no takers.

"What do you think is going to happen?" Dan asked.

They all looked at me.

"Well, if there's blood on the dress, it will have to be analyzed. Which will take at least another day or two at the earliest. If there's a lot of blood on the dress, it will be pretty obvious." I looked at Herbie. "Sorry."

He shrugged his shoulders. "I know Laura. There's not going to be any blood on the dress. We don't even know if the deputy had the dress in the bag."

"That's true," Colin said. "Could have been anything else. Like..." he looked at me for help.

"Josh's shoes. Josh could have had blood on his shoes. Maybe Josh did it," I speculated.

"I would love it if Josh got arrested," Dan said. "That would solve a lot of problems."

"Yeah, the only bad thing about working for Josh is Josh," Colin said.

It broke the tension.

"Who knows," I started. "Fletcher could have brought the bag in with him, expecting to find something and didn't. The bag could have been empty for all we know."

Everyone perked up at that. None of us wanted to acknowledge the obvious.

"Movie?" Colin asked.

"What do you have?"

He flipped open his laptop and read out from a list. A lot of Bond, all of the Bourne movies, some rom-coms.

"I vote for *Princess Bride*," I said.

"Me, too." Dan stood up, brandishing an imaginary sword. "My name is Inigo Montoya. You killed my father. Prepare to die!"

Colin looked at Herbie. "You good with it?"

"Definitely."

We settled in to watch the movie. We'd all seen it multiple times which only added to the enjoyment. It was good to get away from reality for a couple of hours. But we didn't go in for a second movie. The suspicion of Laura being a killer hung over us. We said our good nights a bit awkwardly. Whatever bonding had gone on this weekend had suffered a tear.

I opened up the Lorna Doones after they left and paired it with a hefty amount of scotch. I tried to read my book, but couldn't concentrate. I kept getting up whenever I heard a noise in the hall. Maybe Josh and Laura had returned to their room while we were watching the movie. But I didn't think so. Josh wanted to hang out with the elite. They would have gone into the bar after dinner, Laura miserable while Josh tried desperately to be relevant. Or maybe they were being questioned by Deputy Fletcher right now. I reached for my phone, intending to text Laura and then realized that it wouldn't work.

My curiosity was making me too restless to concentrate. I left half the Lorna Doones and almost all of my scotch and headed down to the lobby. I would just casually pop into the bar for a drink.

You Might Have Mentioned That Earlier

THE BAR WAS FAIRLY full. Obviously, the company dinner had let out and a good number of the VashTech people were making a night of it. It made sense, really. No television, no Internet. The only entertainment was drinking in the lounge.

I took up my spot at the end of the bar and looked around. I saw Laura and Josh on the fringes of a group that had pushed two tables together. They were down one end and most of the conversation didn't seem to involve them. Fletcher hadn't pulled Laura in for questioning yet. Maybe that was good news. Irene and Edward were with Trip and his wife and another couple. Another group seemed to be the "juniors"—younger couples, the wives looking fresh and polished. The younger men had all loosened their ties or taken them off completely. Jackets were off, sleeves rolled up. The older men were all still fully suited. The old guard were not the guys who wore Hawaiian shirts on casual Fridays.

"Orange juice?" Vitor was in front of me.

"I would love a vodka and cranberry."

"Coming right up. Tito's?"

"Whatever's in the well. I honestly can't taste the difference."

He shook his head. I noticed he poured something better than well, but not top shelf. He set it in front of me with a wink, and then turned to take care of one of the servers. Even though the bar wasn't completely full, the crowd was drinking heavily. Vitor and the wait staff were in full swing tonight. I was tempted to watch him as he worked the familiar space behind the bar. Instead, I checked out the room a little more carefully.

There were a few couples who weren't part of the VashTech crowd. I wondered if Fletcher had checked into all the guests to see if any had a connection to Marie Janeé. I didn't know how he would do that, but then, I figured that must be something they teach you in deputy school. That was if he had had time to even do background checks. The Internet had gone down in the storm. And he was just one guy.

For all the alcohol being served, no one was getting too loud or boisterous. Maybe it was out of respect for Marie Janeé, or more likely, for Stephen. Or maybe it was because senior management was in the bar and people were smart enough not to screw up on company turf. I heard a lot of talk of the Bucs and missing out on watching whichever game. Not a lot of shop talk and I was willing to bet that no one was talking about the murder in anything above a whisper. And there was whispering going on.

I was almost done with my drink when Deputy Fletcher came through the door and looked around. He saw me at the bar and walked over.

"Are Laura and Josh in here?"

I nodded. "They're over at the big table, on the end." I didn't want to point but he followed my gaze. "Time to question Laura?"

"Yes. I don't want Josh with her. He's going to intimidate her and frankly, just get in the way."

"That will piss him off."

"Ask me if I care."

I laughed.

"Will you sit in on the questioning? She may say nothing, but I don't want her coming back and saying I bullied her into a confession or I did something, um..."

"That you harassed or propositioned her? Yeah, I'll be there to make sure you don't."

"I wouldn't do that!"

"I know. But she doesn't know that." I shrugged. I signaled Vitor for my tab. "I'll meet you at the event room. Probably better if Josh doesn't know I'm sitting in."

Vitor came over and Fletcher quickly said, "Put it on my tab." Vitor nodded.

"Thanks. You run a tab here?"

"I do this weekend." He made his way over to Laura and Josh and I headed for the door. But I paused to see how Josh would react. As I suspected, it was not well. I heard Fletcher say "The best thing you can do is go wait in your room. In fact, I recommend it highly." I smirked and headed over to the event room.

I understood Fletcher had to question Laura, but I thought he was on the wrong track. The least I could do was stand by Laura while she was questioned. I threw her under the bus. Maybe I could make sure she didn't get flattened.

THE QUESTIONING WAS NOT going well for Laura. Or maybe for Deputy Fletcher. She stuck to her story, but there were a lot of tears. We'd been in the room for over an hour.

"I don't know who killed her. It wasn't me. I saw her in the hall, she was rude and mean, and I went into the ladies' room to change. I didn't see her when I came back out and I was glad she wasn't around. I thought about blowing off the dinner altogether and just going back to the room."

"Did you go back to your room?"

"Well, yes. I dropped off my change of clothes."

"Why didn't you just go up to your room to change in the first place?"

"I was going to drop my clothes back off in the Green Room, but when I went back, the door was locked. I figured Herbie locked it."

"Herbie?" I said. Deputy Fletcher shot a dark look at me.

"He was in the Green Room, packing up his stuff."

"You didn't think to mention this earlier?"

Laura shrugged. "He's almost always the last one out. He's got a lot of equipment."

"How long did it take you to change?"

"A little over fifteen minutes. Maybe closer to twenty."

"To change a dress?"

Laura looked embarrassed. "I spent the first five minutes or so crying. So stupid. It's not like Josh is a great boyfriend. She could have him."

Fletcher looked at me and I shrugged. I didn't disagree with her assessment. I was just surprised that she saw Josh that clearly. Or maybe it was just hindsight, between the lipstick on his collar, his making a pass at Marie Janeé, and his reaction to her pregnancy, he was—at last—losing appeal. Laura might have finally come to the realization that Josh was not good boyfriend material, much less father material. But I doubted that she had been ready to throw him out last night.

"Let me get this right. Herbie was in the Green Room when you went to change. Fifteen minutes later, the door was locked."

"Yes. So, I had to go back up to the room to drop off my stuff."

Fletcher turned to me. "When you and Colin checked the Green Room, was the door locked?"

"No. Otherwise we couldn't have gotten in."

Fletcher nodded. I knew what he was thinking. But he was on the wrong track. Herbie was even more mild-mannered than Laura.

Laura looked wrung out. I didn't blame her.

"Do you need Laura anymore tonight?"

"No. We're done for now. But if you remember anything else..."

She nodded. She got up from the chair and sat back down again.

"Sorry, lightheaded."

Deputy Fletcher handed her a bottled water from his stash. She swallowed a few ounces and sat for a minute. Then she nodded to herself and stood slowly.

"I'll walk you back to the room." I held out my arm and we made our way to the door.

"I'm fine, really. Just so tired."

"I bet."

She didn't speak again until we got to the elevators.

"I am done with Josh. I meant that. I've been making allowances for him all this time. I've been an idiot."

"Love makes us all stupid. Believe me. Are you going to need a place to stay tonight?"

"No. There are two beds. I slept in the other bed last night. I'll let him know it's over once I've figured out a place to move to and get my ducks in a row. So..."

"Just between us girls. I know."

The elevator doors opened and we got out our room keycards. I walked her to her door and she put the keycard up to the reader.

"No need." I pointed to the latch which was flipped around to keep the door ajar.

She swung open the door and we both screamed.

It's Not Paranoia...

I GRABBED LAURA BACK out from the doorway and looked around wildly. I saw Colin's head poke out his door.

"Colin, find Deputy Fletcher and get him up here. He's in the event room."

I must have looked as freaked out as I felt because Colin ran to the elevators and stabbed the button. He waited a few seconds, then decided to take the stairs.

Herbie's door opened and he came out. "What's wrong?"

"Josh is dead." I said quietly. I could hear Laura gagging beside me. "Get Laura into your room, would you?"

Herbie came to where we were and took Laura's arm.

One of the VashTech executives came into the hallway and a few other doors opened up just enough to listen in.

"What's all the noise about?"

"Sorry, um, my friend drank too much and we got silly. We'll keep it down."

"Make sure you do."

Herbie led Laura down to his room. She was unsteady on her feet and leaned heavily against Herbie. Doors closed one by one. Nothing to see except a couple of inebriated women. I waited for all the doors to shut and then used my elbow to swing the door open again. I forced myself to look. Josh was on the floor, face down. He looked like he had tumbled out of the chair. His arms were by his sides, which was weird. Normally when you fall, your arms go out to protect yourself. Maybe he wasn't dead. Should I check to see if he had a pulse? I took a couple of steps into the room and the door automatically soft-closed against the latch. I tried to be careful where I stepped, but there was no blood. I knelt down beside him and felt the knee of my jeans grow damp.

I jumped back and looked at the floor. No blood. Just wet for some reason. Then I saw the empty water bottle on the floor. Very glad I hadn't knelt in pee.

I squatted down and picked up his wrist, feeling for a pulse. Nothing. But he was still warm. His eyes were open, bulging slightly. I didn't know if he had been strangled or if it was his normal angry face. His neck didn't appear to have any bruises on it. I backed away from the body. I covered my hand with my shirt sleeve and slipped through the door, back into the hall.

The elevator dinged. Colin must have found Deputy Fletcher pretty fast. I looked down the hall and saw Dan step out. He was carrying a rolled-up sheaf of papers.

"Hey, whatcha doin'?"

"Shhh."

"What?"

"Josh is dead," I whispered.

"Whoa!" He took a second to absorb the news. "Is Laura okay?"

"She's in with Herbie."

"We need to get that deputy."

"I sent Colin. Where are you coming from?"

"I took a walk. Trying to learn my lines for a new show I'm cast in." He waved the roll of papers.

"Did you see anyone in the hallway?"

"No. But I've been gone for almost an hour."

"Did you notice if Josh's door was open? You know, with the latch flipped over."

"I didn't even look. I just headed to the elevators. Maybe Herbie or Colin saw something."

Herbie. Shit. A succession of thoughts flipped through my mind and they weren't good. Herbie was in the Green Room when Marie Janeé was killed and now he was just a few doors down from Josh's room. Could be a coincidence. I needed to give that more thought, but now was not the time.

"Go knock on Herbie's door and see how Laura's doing. I have to wait for the Deputy. And can you call security from there?"

"Sure." He made a move as if he wanted to see what was in the room.

"You don't want to see it," I said.

"You're right. I wasn't thinking." He moved down to Herbie's room and knocked.

I heard Herbie say, "Come on in, man." Then he poked his head out. "What's going on?"

"Waiting for Colin and the deputy. How's Laura?"

Herbie stepped into the hallway. "She's in the bathroom, hurling. Doesn't want me in there with her. What should I do?"

"Let her be. She's had a lot of experience at this lately," I said. "Maybe find her some saltines."

He nodded.

"Can you prop your door open? I figure we're all going to be in your room soon."

"Sure."

I wanted to make sure nothing would happen to Dan or Laura. I didn't think Herbie was a murderer, but I have nothing against being paranoid, either.

I stood outside Josh's room, waiting for what seemed forever. The elevator dinged again and Deputy Fletcher, a security guard and Colin stepped out. Fletcher led the way down the hall, the other two trailing behind. He looked at me and I pointed to the door.

"The latch was like that when we got here. Laura and I started to go in and, well, you can see for yourself."

Fletcher and the security guard entered the room. I heard a short curse and then Fletcher told the security guard to stand back. They both came out of the room and Fletcher sighed.

"Well, you and Laura are in the clear on this one."

"No kidding."

He looked at the security guard. "Ask the manager for the names and room numbers of everyone on this hall. He'll probably want to be up here, too." The guard moved a bit down the hallway and got on his walkie-talkie.

"We're all in the closest rooms." I started to indicate the rooms but Fletcher had already searched most of them. Dan was standing in Herbie's doorway, watching what was going on. All the other room doors were closed. I wondered how many eyes were at peepholes. "There's water or something on the floor by the body." I pointed to my damp knee. He nodded.

"Where's Laura?"

"She's in Herbie's room," I pointed to where Dan was standing. "Not doing too well."

He nodded. "You may as well go and wait there with the group." He looked at the security guard. "Hey, Artie."

Artie came back to the room and took up a position outside the door. Fletcher went back inside the room and I went down to join my colleagues. The thought of stopping by my room to grab the scotch flitted through my mind. I was feeling a little queasy after seeing Josh, and I wasn't sure if alcohol would help or hurt.

Dan drew aside to let me in and then closed the door behind us. I could hear Laura in the bathroom. She wasn't vomiting but she was crying. Herbie and Colin were sitting at the little table. Dan chose one of the beds and I went in to check on Laura.

I handed her the box of tissues. "Feel ready to come out?"

"I'm not sure. My mouth is disgusting."

I looked at Herbie's sink area and grabbed a tube of toothpaste. "Rinse your mouth and then put some of this in there." I helped her stand and she hunched over the sink, using her hand to cup water to her mouth.

"I am so tired of throwing up. My ribs hurt."

"You've done more than your share lately."

I handed her the toothpaste. She squeezed out a bit on her finger and ran it around her mouth. She rinsed and repeated.

"Is everyone out there?"

"Yeah."

She nodded and squared her shoulders. "Okay then."

We joined the others in the main room. Herbie jumped up and offered Laura the chair then he sat on the bed closest to her. I joined Colin on the other bed. There was an awkward silence. Colin finally broke it.

"Sorry about Josh, Laura."

Herbie and Dan chimed in. Laura looked like she was going to start crying again, but managed to swallow it down.

"Who would want to kill Josh?" she asked in a small voice. The guys and I exchanged looks. I hoped my look conveyed to them not to give the obvious answer.

"It may be natural causes," I said. "It looks like he was sitting in the chair and maybe, I don't know, had a heart attack, and fell out of the chair."

"Did Josh have a heart condition?" Colin asked Laura.

She looked confused. "I don't think so. Do you think it was the stress of me being pregnant and Marie Janeé being murdered? He was so upset that it would reflect badly on the company."

We were silent for a few seconds, thinking it through. Herbie spoke first.

"Maybe Josh killed Marie Janeé and felt guilty about it and killed himself."

Colin looked at me. "Did you see a note?"

"No. But I could have missed it." I thought back. The table had the normal room service menu and flyers on it. Josh's phone was by the chair he'd fallen from. I shook my head.

Dan wasn't going to let the idea of murder go. "Maybe it's just meant to look like natural causes. Or a suicide."

"It's a possibility. I mean, Josh suddenly keeling over is pretty coincidental," Colin said.

"If so, it's got to be tied into Marie Janeé's murder somehow," I said. "There must be something we don't know about their relationship."

"When did it happen?" Dan asked.

I thought back. Laura, the Deputy and I all left the lounge at the same time. Josh could have gone back to his room then. Sometime in the hour or so that we were with Deputy Fletcher, someone had met up with Josh in his room.

"Probably in the last hour and a half," I said. "Laura and I were with Deputy Fletcher for just over an hour. We came straight back up to the room. Did you guys hear anyone knock on Josh's door?"

Colin and Herbie shook their heads.

"I might have been gone at that point," Dan said. "I was down near the pool and workout areas."

"Did anyone see you there?"

"What? Do you think I killed Josh?"

"Of course not. But you're going to need an alibi. All three of you."

The guys looked at each other uncomfortably.

"Crap," Colin said. "I was just watching another movie on my laptop."

"I was repacking my equipment to go home tomorrow. I figure it's still going to be a rough crossing and I wanted everything well-padded."

Laura turned pale and I watched her struggle to keep whatever was left in her stomach down.

"There's something else we need to think about," Colin said.

"What's that?" Herbie asked.

"We're not just suspects. We could also be targets."

"Yeah. Maybe someone hates actors or something," Dan said.

"Again, possible. But not probable. I think this has more to do with Marie Janeé and Josh than us. So, other than Stephen Vashon, who would have it in for them?"

"You said the bartender used to date Marie Janeé. Maybe he was jealous?" Herbie offered.

"He was working the bar when we left, but that doesn't mean he couldn't have taken a break." I thought about it. "I think he had an alibi for Marie Janeé's death. But he could have seen Josh leaving the bar and followed him to his room."

"Okay, so that's two possibilities. Who else?" Dan asked.

I shrugged. "Someone we don't know. Maybe someone knew Marie Janeé and Josh when they were doing shows together. Kind of a long-shot coincidence thing."

"Could be one of us," Colin said.

"You mean one of you three guys?" I laughed, but it was just for show. None of them had an alibi for Josh's murder. And Herbie didn't really have an alibi for Marie Janeé's murder.

"Well, not for killing Marie Janeé, but I would have been more than happy to slap Josh around on several occasions." Colin looked at Laura. "Sorry, Laura."

"It's okay. He could be a total jerk."

"I didn't like the way he picked on everyone," Herbie said. "Maybe he was rude to the wrong person."

"People don't usually kill someone who's rude to them," Dan countered.

"What if Josh doubled back to apologize to you?" I asked Laura. "Maybe he went back to the Green Room and saw Marie Janeé or saw whoever killed her coming out of the Green Room?"

"Wouldn't he have said something to Deputy Fletcher?" Herbie asked.

Laura looked around at us. "We kind of fibbed to Deputy Fletcher. We agreed it was better if we just said what everyone else was saying—that we left the Meet and Greet and went straight into dinner."

"But now Fletcher knows that you didn't."

"Did you see Josh again before you went to the dinner?"

"No. He said he went straight into the dinner and I had no reason not to believe him."

"So, Josh could have been lying, too. Maybe there was a reason why he was eager to give you an alibi."

Sheesh. I could see what Deputy Fletcher meant about people lying to him all the time.

"Josh might have realized that he saw the murderer. If he figured out who killed Marie Janeé and accused them..." Colin started slowly.

"And they killed him so they wouldn't be found out!" Dan finished. He jumped up from the bed in excitement.

"Why wouldn't he have gone to Deputy Fletcher as soon as he figured it out?" I asked. "That doesn't make sense."

"Unless he thought he could blackmail the killer," Dan said. I just looked at him. He really had a wild imagination.

"Josh is a lot of things, but I don't think he'd be brave enough to blackmail a killer," Colin said.

I thought about it. "He was trying to raise money to buy a restaurant or catering hall. Did you know about that Laura?"

"Yeah. He had found a few places, but last week he found one that would be perfect. His heart was kind of set on it. Maybe that's why he didn't take the news of the baby so well." She started crying again.

"That would mean Marie Janeé's killer had a lot of money."

"One of the VashTech executives."

"Who do you think Josh accused?" Herbie asked.

We all looked at each other.

"Could be anybody," Dan said. He sat back down again.

"I wonder if he made any notes," Colin looked at Laura.

"I don't think so. He would have dictated them to me. Just to feel important."

We nodded. That would be Josh. He wouldn't even think that he might be hurting Laura's feelings.

"But he knew Marie Janeé from before and he may have known Vitor, the bartender. So, Laura, was there anyone else here that he mentioned he knew?"

"He didn't mention it, but he did seem to know one of the other VashTech execs. One of the younger guys."

"Okay. Okay. That's something. Could you point him out to us if you saw him again, Laura?" Dan was excited again. I wondered if it was the actor in him that made all his reactions over the top, or if his ability to react was what led him to become an actor. Or maybe that was just Dan.

"Yeah, probably." She looked at me. "He was one of the guys at the table with us in the bar. The one with the reddish-brown hair? Tall."

They'd all been sitting, so I was basically drawing a blank. I shook my head. "Don't remember him, but as long as you do, that will work."

"Maybe we should go down to the bar and see if he's still there."

"I think Deputy Fletcher wants us to stay here."

"Yeah, but he could be hours," Dan said.

"Let's go. One quick drink, we'll see if the guy is there, and then we come back up." This from Herbie.

"We can raise a glass to Josh," Colin said, looking at me.

"I don't know why you think you need my permission. But yeah, let's go. Fletcher can find us if he needs us. Are you up for this, Laura?"

"Not for the drinking part. But I can point him out to you. Then maybe I can get some crackers at the gift shop or the restaurant."

We gathered ourselves up to go.

Dan swung open the door. "We drink to Josh!"

Deputy Fletcher was standing in the hall. "No drinking yet. I'm going to need to talk to all of you." He looked at the guys. "Especially you three."

Lorna Doones Can Only Do So Much

We shifted back into the room and Deputy Fletcher closed the door. Laura and I took the chairs at the little table and the three guys sat on one bed, all in a row, looking like they were See No Evil, Hear No Evil, Speak No Evil.

Fletcher leaned against the bureau. "I'll get right to it. I need your whereabouts for the last two and half hours."

"So, not natural causes then?" I asked.

"He was held down and smothered. There were fibers in his nose and mouth from one of the pillows. And bruises on his chest from where he was pinned down. I need to know where you three were."

He wasn't particularly happy with the answers he got. None of the guys had a good alibi. But probably half the people in the hotel didn't have one, either. He looked at Dan's running shoes.

"Why are your shoes wet?"

"I stepped outside for a minute or two, just trying to get some fresh air. We've been stuck in here for two days. I stood under the roof part of the outside pool."

"And you were learning your lines in the dark?"

"No, I went down to the pool area. I need to pace when I'm learning my lines and I can't do that in these rooms. Three steps and I'm at the door." He paused and looked at us, checking for agreement of some sort. "So, I went down to the back hallway by the pool. It's long enough to pace and no one is down there at this hour. It sounded like the rain was letting up, so I stepped outside to clear my head. I came back in, worked some more, and then came back to my room. And I saw Kasey in the hall, waiting for you."

"Did anyone see you down there?"

"I don't know. I don't think so. I mean, I went there so I wouldn't be disturbed."

Fletcher made a few notes on his pad, nodded but didn't say anything.

"You've got to believe me!"

"I don't have to believe you. The rug was damp underneath the body. But your feet are way too big to match the partial shoe indent we found."

"For Pete's sake, Fletcher, why pick on the kid then?" I glared at him. "It was probably my boot."

"I wasn't picking on him. I was hoping he might have seen something. Which he didn't." He closed the cover of the pad. "And it wasn't your boot, either." He switched gears. "Why were you all going down to the bar?"

"Laura said she thought Josh might have known one of the VashTech guys from somewhere else. She was going to point him out to us."

Fletcher looked at Laura. "You didn't think to mention this?"

"Obviously not. And you didn't ask."

Fletcher took that last bit better than I thought he would.

"Rather than having all five of you go trooping into the lounge and then staring at someone who might be a suspect, maybe you should have brought that piece of information to me."

"Well, we were going to be subtle," Colin said. He pronounced subtle in the British way.

"I saw your show. Subtle is not in your repertoire."

He didn't say it for the laugh, but Dan elbowed Colin. "Good one. He got you."

"I was serious," Fletcher protested.

It didn't matter. It relieved a bit of the tension.

"So, do you want Laura to go to the lounge with you and see if the guy is still there?" I asked.

"Yes. I think just the two of us would be a little more... subtle." He pronounced it the way Colin had. "We're going to need to get you a different room for the night. We'll stop by the front desk."

Laura stood up to go, but Fletcher wasn't done with us.

"None of you go anywhere alone. Stay in pairs at minimum. We don't know who is behind this, but it looks like it is more related to your group than to VashTech."

My stomach did a little flip. The guys were uncharacteristically quiet.

"I'll escort Laura back up here. We're going to lock down the room. The storm is letting up. Lee County should be able to get a forensics team over here tomorrow."

"Are you leaving Josh's body in the room?" I asked in surprise.

"Yes. The EMTs could get through to take the body down to the station, but the roads are still pretty dangerous. I don't want to have to mount a rescue mission in the middle of this. If Josh were injured, it would be a different story. It's best to leave the body in place. We'll have someone posted outside the room all night."

"I'll need to get my things," Laura said.

"I can go in and do that for you when we come back up. Just tell me what to get."

Laura nodded.

Fletcher and Laura left, and the second the door closed Dan fell backwards on the bed.

"Criminy! I thought I was going to get arrested. All I did was walk outside for a minute!"

"Good thing you've got big feet," Colin teased him.

"Isn't it kind of weird that they're just leaving Josh's body there?" Herbie asked.

"Creepy," Dan agreed.

"There was no point in risking the EMTs having an accident. Josh is dead."

Colin looked at me. "That makes sense. But it's still weird."

"This whole thing is weird," I said. "What are the odds that we get stuck in a storm and two people get murdered? If Fletcher is right, the murderer knew Josh and Marie Janeé from a few years back."

"Somebody from their old acting days?" Colin asked.

"Or from that business club up in Tampa where Marie Janeé worked," Herbie said.

"I don't think so. Josh wasn't in that circle."

"So, more likely, someone who was an actor or some sort of performer and worked with both of them," Dan said. "We can't ask Josh."

"The one time he would have been useful," Colin noted.

We were silent.

"Did any of you work with Josh when Marie Janeé was with the company?" I was the newest addition to the troupe.

"That was a couple of years back, at least," Colin said. "I've only been with the troupe for about a year. Dan, you were here when I came in."

Dan nodded.

"I think I've been with Josh the longest. I was working with him before Laura joined," Herbie volunteered.

"Back in the *Dracula* days?" Dan asked.

"I came just after Marie Janeé left, I guess." Herbie assessed Dan. "You would have made a good Dracula."

"That was part of the reason I joined the troupe. Then Josh cut the show. I was pretty disappointed."

"Well, you at least got to wear the Dracula cape a few times."

Dan looked at him, not understanding.

"Marley's cape. That was the Dracula cape."

"Cool!"

"It's ruined now," I said. Marie Janeé's body had been lying on top of it in the prop trunk. "Wait. Doesn't the cape usually get hung up and kept with the hats? Not in the prop trunk? Whoever killed Marie Janeé could have been wearing the cape. That's why they weren't covered in blood."

I saw realization dawn on Dan's face. "Aw, man. The cape is ruined."

So, not realization. I looked at Herbie. His eyes were wide. He got it. So did Colin.

"Did we hang up the cape?" I asked.

"I'm pretty sure it was there," Herbie said. The two hat boxes were still on the prop table. I finished packing up my stuff. Laura came in to get the garment bag. I could tell she was upset."

"We could ask Laura if she remembers the cape being hung up next to her garment bag."

"Did you hear Laura and Marie Janeé in the hall way?" I asked.

"No. Laura said she would lock up. I figured she might change in the Green Room, so I went out through the event room. It's faster, anyway."

I nodded, but I didn't like it. The timing was just too tight.

Colin was thinking out loud. "Herbie leaves. Laura takes the garment bag, heads out of the Green Room to go change. Runs into Marie Janeé. They have that nasty little scene." He paused. "Maybe Josh did come back, heard what was going on. Maybe he lured her into the Green Room, he hits her and knocks her out. Now he's hit the client..."

Dan picked it up. "If Marie Janeé tells her husband, that's it. Game over for Josh. So, he thinks fast, puts on the cape, grabs an icicle off the tree, and bam."

We sat quietly, thinking of the icicle in Marie Janeé's chest.

"That's if Josh came back. And knowing Josh, do you think he would have missed out on a minute of hobnobbing with big wigs to go apologize to Laura?"

Dan shook his head. "No way."

"It's possible, but not probable," Colin said.

"It does seem out of character," Herbie started, "but maybe he's nicer to Laura in private than he is in public. I mean, there's got to be a reason that she stays with him. Though I can't figure it out."

"Herbie, we need to face a few facts." I said it as gently as possible. "There's a good chance that Laura killed Marie Janeé."

"Then who killed Josh?" he countered.

Nobody had an answer.

"C'mon you guys. We know Laura. She doesn't have it in her to kill anyone."

"Do you think I could kill someone?" I asked, testing the waters.

"Oh, hell yeah," Dan didn't hesitate. The other two nodded in agreement.

"Thanks a bunch!" It broke the tension a bit. "Seriously?"

"Well, you're a whole lot more likely than Laura, that's for sure," Colin said.

"I could see you killing Josh," Dan nodded to himself.

"Fortunately, I have an alibi. And you don't."

Dan lifted up his foot. "I don't fit the description."

I thought back to Josh hitting on Marie Janeé. "Josh never got over his feelings for Marie Janeé."

"Well, he's been living with Laura for at least a year," Dan said. "I thought they were happy together."

"Laura's a pretty woman, but look at her and look at Marie Janeé," I said. "And Marie Janeé could sing and dance as well as act. Laura was in a no-win situation. When Josh said she looked like a second-rate Marie Janeé, he was saying more about himself than Laura."

"He was looking for a Marie Janeé replacement," Dan said.

"I think Laura is prettier than Marie Janeé," Herbie said. "And definitely the better person. She was actually too good for Josh."

"You've got that right," Colin agreed. He imitated Forrest Gump: "Pretty is as pretty does."

"But I think Herbie is right. I don't think Laura could kill anyone," Dan said. "But Josh could."

We nodded. I didn't think Laura had killed Marie Janeé, but I didn't think Josh had, either. I had my own theory working.

"What's going to happen to the company? Do you think Laura will run it?" Herbie asked.

"I guess so," Colin said.

"If she does, will you guys stay on? I mean, Laura's going to need all the help she can get." Herbie looked at us expectantly.

"Yes, of course," I said quickly.

"It will be a lot more pleasant to work with Laura, for sure," Dan said. Colin nodded in agreement.

We sat, all of us starting to understand the repercussions of Josh's death.

"What if she doesn't want to run the company?" I asked. "I mean, she's pregnant, her baby's father was just murdered..."

"Maybe we shouldn't bring it up to her right away," Colin said. "I'm pretty sure it's the last thing on her mind. Agreed?"

We all nodded.

"I'm going to head off to bed. It's been a big night." I got out of the chair.

"I'll walk you down to your room," Colin volunteered.

"It's two doors down. I think I'm good. But thank you."

I stepped into the hallway. Artie was sitting in a chair outside Josh's room. Colin watched me from the doorway and made sure I got into my room. I gave him a little wave as I went in.

I checked the bathroom and the closet and then under the beds. No boogeymen. I looked at the glass of scotch on the nightstand and made a beeline for it. Lorna Doones are good, but they can only do so much.

I sat at the little table with paper and pen and scotch and cookies. The paper and pen were to help me organize my thoughts. The scotch was to help me take a hard look at Herbie as a suspect. I don't need a reason to eat Lorna Doones.

It was hard to think of Herbie as a killer, but I forced myself to be objective. He was the only one who didn't want to quit the troupe after Josh had yelled at us. Herbie and Laura, really. Laura wouldn't quit because she was involved with Josh. That made sense. I wrote down "Why would Herbie stay?" and underlined it and then I answered my own question. "Why not?" It wasn't a bad gig from his point of view and while Josh was inconsiderate, he didn't bully Herbie the same way he bullied cast members. On the other hand, Josh was barely polite to Herbie. Maybe Herbie was just used to being treated like that. And mostly, he worked with Laura, not Josh.

My glass was empty and I got up to refill it. There was a soft knock on my door. I looked through the peephole. Colin's face filled my view.

I opened the door and he slid in quickly, glancing over his shoulder.

"What's up?"

"Shh. Not so loud."

"Why?"

"I don't want anyone to know I'm in here."

"Considering someone is going around murdering us, I'd kind of like people to know you're in here."

He looked confused and then hurt.

"Kidding. Scotch?" I held up the bottle.

"Yes, please."

I poured us both generous amounts. It had been a very bad day. We took our drinks over to the little table. He looked at my notes.

"Herbie? Really?"

"I know. I'm grasping at straws."

"Maybe. Maybe not. That's why I came by. We're obviously thinking along the same lines." He pointed at one of my notes. "I can answer that one for you. Herbie has a crush on Laura."

"No!"

"Yeah."

"That's so cute."

"Well, it would be except we find out Laura's pregnant and Josh is dead hours later."

"Good point."

"Do we really know him? I mean, really, outside of going out after a show, we haven't hung out with him until this weekend. And we're always in a large group. What do you really know about him?"

I took a slow sip of my scotch. "Not much. Plus, the timeline is too tight. Herbie says he left the Green Room before Laura which might be true. She says he was in the Green Room when she left. So, he could have heard Marie Janeé in the hallway. They were right outside the Green Room door. He starts to leave, hears Marie Janeé insult Laura. If he has a crush on Laura..." I let it hang.

"Fifteen minutes later when she went to drop off her first dress in there, the door was locked so she had to go up to her room and leave it there."

"Herbie knew Marie Janeé from before. He could have said something to get her into the Green Room."

He nodded. "If Herbie overheard Marie Janeé being mean to Laura…"

"And then he heard us talking about Josh being mean to her," I trailed off. "But is being mean a motive for murder? Seems pretty weak."

"Marie Janeé was pretty brutal, wasn't she? I mean, if someone is mean to me, I don't like it, but I can handle it. If someone is mean to someone I care about, I kind of go into protection mode."

"Wouldn't Herbie want Marie Janeé around? I mean, if she was a threat to Josh and Laura's relationship, that would be good for him."

Colin thought about that. "Maybe. Or maybe he just lost it. I mean, who stabs someone with a Christmas ornament? That's not premeditated."

We sat in silence.

Colin tried to play devil's advocate. "It seems like a jump for Herbie to kill Marie Janeé. But if he was in the Green Room, he had opportunity. And access to the weapon."

"Yeah, but he was sitting at dinner with you guys when I walked in. I didn't see any blood on him."

"Okay, let's look at the timeline. Dan and I took about fifteen minutes to change and then went back downstairs. Herbie came into the dining room after we did. At least five minutes later."

"And I came in after that."

"Fletcher checked our shoes."

"Fletcher checked our *elf* shoes. He didn't check all our shoes."

Colin shrugged. "I just have my runners. How many pairs of shoes did you bring?"

"You are so not a girl. I have a pair of heels with me to go with the dress I had for the Meet and Greet, but we didn't change for that. I have my running shoes for just walking around. I have a pair of loafers and my cowboy boots in case I want to go hang out in the bar or if we had been permitted into the dining room."

"For one weekend?"

"I'm a girl. I would bet that Dan and Herbie only brought one pair of street shoes—the ones they're wearing. So, Deputy Fletcher wouldn't have checked those."

"Because he didn't know that Herbie was still in the Green Room..." He looked up. "You think there's blood on Herbie's shoes?"

"There was a lot of blood in the Green Room. And whoever killed Josh stepped in the water."

"Well, if Herbie killed Josh, he probably had time to dry his shoes. And would an imprint last when the water dried?"

I made a face. "Maybe Fletcher got a picture of it. But Marie Janeé's murder doesn't make sense. If Herbie killed her, he would have had blood on his clothes and he didn't change after the show."

"He was really neat?" Colin drank some more scotch. "I know, lame. He could have used the cape."

"Hey, Marie Janeé, I'm going to stab you but first let me cover up? I don't see that happening."

"What if he got her in the Green Room, maybe asked a question about working with Josh, pointed out the Dracula cape. Maybe he puts it on like they're play acting?" Colin wasn't so sure.

"I guess he could have. Let's go through it. Starting with Josh telling Laura to change her dress."

"So, Laura goes back to the Green Room. Gets her other dress. She sees Herbie. He leaves through the event room door. Or says he does." Colin corrected himself.

"She goes back out towards the ladies' room to change and runs into Marie Janeé."

"Who is a snotty wench to her."

"Laura goes into the ladies' room. Cries, changes. That takes at least fifteen minutes. She goes back to the Green Room but it's locked. So, she goes up to her room to drop off her stuff. Did you see her when you left your room?"

"No. Dan and I went down to the dining room together. We didn't see her up here or in the lobby."

"Maybe she spent more time in her room than she said. Took some time to re-do her makeup."

"Meanwhile, Herbie has somehow enticed Marie Janeé into the Green Room and killed her." Colin sounded frustrated. "How does he get her into the Green Room?"

"Wait a minute. Marie Janeé used to do shows with Josh and really, not that long ago. Like maybe three years or so?" I looked to Colin for confirmation on the time frame. "How long have you been with Josh?"

"Two years. I came after Marie Janeé had left. But Herbie was already part of the troupe when I joined.

Everybody lies.

"Maybe Herbie lied. They knew each other."

"You'd think he would have mentioned it," Colin said.

"Not if he killed her."

"Good point."

"We need to go see Deputy Fletcher."

I grabbed my keycard and we went out into the hall.

"Isn't the security guy supposed to be here?" I whispered.

"Yeah. He wasn't there when I came down to your room. I figured he had to go to the bathroom."

"It's been a while. Maybe more than a bathroom break."

We passed by the empty chair. The room door was shut tight.

"Should we knock?"

"I don't think Deputy Fletcher is in there. What's more worrying is that the security guy is missing. Besides, I don't want heads popping out of doorways." I indicated Herbie's room with a nod.

"Gotcha."

No Apologies Necess—Ah, Yeah.

We found Fletcher in his temporary office. He looked up at us with a sigh.

"It's late." He looked at Colin. "And you're a suspect."

"We've got a better suspect. But you need to know your security guy is missing," I said.

This got his attention. Fletcher jumped up. "What?"

"Artie wasn't in the hall. There was no one there."

He grabbed his walkie-talkie, called out to Artie. There was no answer. We followed him out of the room to the elevators.

We rode up in silence, with the exception of Fletcher's teeth grinding. The hallway was still empty when we made the turn from the elevators. Fletcher got a keycard out of his badge pocket and unlocked the door. He went through the door and we followed, uninvited. He glanced back. "Don't touch anything."

Josh's body was where it had been earlier, but something didn't look right to me. I squinted at it but that didn't tell me anything.

Fletcher quickly glanced around the room and then looked into the bathroom. Artie was on the floor, bound and gagged, and conscious.

Fletcher pulled out his pocket knife and quickly removed the gag, then the ties on his hands and feet.

"Are you okay?"

"They knocked me over the head. Sorry, Travis."

"No reason to apologize. Who's they?"

"Maybe not they. Maybe just one person. I don't know. I might have drifted off sitting there."

That explained the need to apologize, I thought.

"It's not like we've had a lot of sleep over the past thirty-six hours." Fletcher helped him up. "Let's see if anyone in the hotel can take a look at your head." He looked at Colin. "Help me get him to the chair outside."

While Fletcher was calling down to the front desk, I looked around the room. I couldn't shake the feeling that something wasn't right, but I didn't know what it was. Fletcher came back in.

"You took pictures earlier, yeah?" I asked.

"Yeah. Why?"

"Something's different."

He pulled out his digital camera and started flipping through the pictures. Most were extreme close ups of the wounds. I stopped him when he got to a picture of the entire scene. "There."

"Son of a gun."

Before I could say anything else, Fletcher was in the hallway. "Artie, did you touch the body at all? Move the arms?"

"No way, man. I didn't want to go near it. I was getting the creeps just sitting out in the hall."

Fletcher grunted. The elevator doors dinged and the night manager came down the hall with a first aid kit.

"Jeez, Artie. What the hell happened?" The night manager examined the top of Artie's head. "I don't know how to stitch anyone up."

"Is there anything in there for this headache?" Artie asked.

The manager started digging.

"He needs acetaminophen, not Ibuprofen. And if you can get an icebag going, it's going to help a lot."

"You have medical training?" The night manager looked relieved.

"No. Just taken a few hits to the head."

Fletcher threw me a questioning glance before getting down to handling the situation. "Maybe you can take him down to the office. It's late and we might be disturbing the guests. Artie, I'll be down in a few to debrief."

Artie nodded and let the manager walk him to the elevators.

Fletcher looked up and down the hallway. "You two come in here. I'm pretty sure people are watching."

Colin hesitated at the doorway. "Maybe we could talk in Kasey's or my room."

I gave Colin my keycard. "Help yourself to the scotch."

Fletcher and I went back in the room and stood near the body.

"Why would someone move his arms?" I asked.

"To get to his pockets." Fletcher pointed at one of the pockets with the toe of his boot. "You can see where they rolled him a bit to get to the other pocket."

"I take it you had already checked his pockets?"

"Yes. Wallet, room key card, some change, his cell phone."

"That's it?"

"Yeah. Time to do a closer check on his wallet and cell phone."

"Where are they?"

"I've got them locked up with the rest of the evidence. At this point, we're using two safes, plus one of the hotel rooms."

"Can't the maids get in?"

"No, we changed the code so the housekeeping keys can't override the system. Only the manager, Artie, and I can get in."

"Did you do the same thing to Josh's room? Change the code?"

"Absolutely." Realization hit him. "Shit. Artie's key card."

"That's how they got into the room. And why he was knocked over the head."

"Let's go." Fletcher locked the door to Josh's room, and then let out a sigh of disgust. "Listen, don't stand in the hallway, but can you and Colin keep an eye on this door from your room? I've got to go down, make sure the evidence room hasn't been tampered with, and then recode everything. I'll be back up as soon as I can."

"Got it."

I went back to my room. Colin had skipped my scotch in favor of a beer. I was glad he hadn't found my stash of Twizzlers. I flipped the latch on the door so we could keep an eye on Josh's room through the open crack. I waved him over.

"What's up?"

I explained about the key cards.

"Man, Fletcher is cooked if someone got into the evidence."

"If they got into the evidence, it means they knew what room it was in. How many rooms in this hotel? Eighty?"

"I guess."

"So, if they got into the evidence room, whoever "they" are, it means they knew about it and they knew where it was. Which means it's someone at the hotel."

"Maybe not Herbie?" Colin was hopeful.

"That would be very good," I said. I liked Herbie. I would also hate for my instincts to be so far off. It did not bode well for my survival.

Colin considered this new information. "Fletcher had Josh's room recoded, which means Laura's key card wouldn't have worked if she had tried to go back in."

"Yeah, and she would have had to get past Artie. So maybe she goes back to the room, tells Artie she needs something, tries her keycard and it doesn't work."

"And, Artie being helpful, whips the new keycard out of his pocket, explains that it's been recoded, and escorts her into the room and back out again."

"In which case, Laura would have known her keycard wouldn't work and that Artie had a pass card."

Colin shook his head. "But I doubt Laura could have hit Artie over the head."

"Maybe she told Herbie." A very bad thought occurred to me. "What if Laura and Herbie are in it together?" I felt a chill run through me.

"You think you know people..." Colin began.

"I almost offered to let Laura stay in my room tonight. I have got to get better at reading people."

"We could be jumping to conclusions."

"I hope so. There's one way to find out. Whoever has that keycard is the person who hit Artie over the head and went through Josh's pockets."

Colin looked at me. "Someone went through his pockets?"

I nodded.

"After he was dead?"

"After we had found the body, notified Fletcher, and had the room sealed." I told him how Josh's arms had been moved to gain access to his pockets.

"So, what was in Josh's pockets? Fletcher would have taken any important stuff like his wallet and cell phone," Colin said.

"Even the unimportant stuff. Did whoever it was think that Josh had something hidden that Fletcher would have missed?"

"It would have to be someone who knows Josh very well." Colin's voice was flat.

"Laura."

"Yeah."

"I don't get what it could be, though." It didn't make any sense to me.

"What if they weren't checking his pockets to take something out? What if they were putting something in?"

"Like what?"

Colin shook his head. "We won't know until we check his pockets. Well, until Fletcher does. I didn't want to go near Josh when he was alive. Dead doesn't make him any more appealing."

I nodded. We waited by the door as the minutes ticked by. I heard the elevator ding and Fletcher turned the corner into our hallway. I stepped out.

"We need to go back into the room." I told him Colin's idea—that maybe something had been placed in Josh's pocket.

Fletcher sighed and pulled a pair of latex gloves from his back pocket. I stood just inside the doorway while Fletcher went into Josh's pockets. He pulled a piece of string from the right front pocket and held it up.

"Blood."

I stepped forward to get a closer look. "Could you have missed that the first time through?"

"Possibly. I mean, pockets have lint and threads. But this is heavier than a thread. I don't think I would have missed it." He fished a glassine envelope out of his breast pocket and dropped the bloody string in, then sealed it.

"You're pretty tired. And overworked," I pointed out.

"Yeah. That's when mistakes are made. So, I could have screwed up and missed it."

"I think that's the string to the ornament. The icicle ornament."

"Interesting."

I gave him a questioning look.

"Let's get out of here."

I watched Fletcher double check that the door was locked.

"Not going to post anyone at the door?" I asked.

"Closing the barn door after the horse has left," he said. "I changed the code again. Someone wants to get in, they're going to make a lot of noise. But I don't think they need to get in anymore."

Colin had been watching us from the room.

"I'm going to grab the bourbon from my room. I'll be right back."

I left the door on the latch and Fletcher sat down at the table. I looked at my diminishing supply of scotch. Still, my mother brought me up right.

"Scotch?"

"Probably shouldn't."

"I've got some Sam Adams in the fridge."

He nodded to that. I crossed over to the fridge and twisted the cap off the bottle before handing it to him. I'm an accomplished hostess.

Fletcher knocked back a long swallow. "I needed that."

I took a sip of my scotch. "Tell me about it."

Colin came back through the door with his bourbon and a glass. "Do you want me to leave the door cracked?"

"No. Close it," Fletcher said. "In fact, we probably shouldn't even be speaking above a whisper at this point."

Colin sat on the bed and looked at us. "Did you find something?"

Fletcher took the envelope out of his pocket and held it up. "What do you think it is?"

"Bloody piece of string." Colin looked at it more closely. "Could it have come from…"

"That's what I thought," I cut in.

"Which means the murderer took the time to remove the string from the ornament after Marie Janeé was killed to make it look like the prop icicle," Fletcher said.

"And to implicate someone in the troupe?" I asked.

"Maybe."

"Or maybe the hotel's ornament was substituted for the prop icicle," Fletcher said flatly. "Someone kills Marie Janeé with the prop icicle and then replaces it with one from the nearest tree."

"So, the icicle in Marie Janeé is not the murder weapon."

"But our icicle wasn't in the prop trunk," Colin said.

Fletcher rubbed his forehead. "Great. Two bodies. No murder weapon. Delayed forensics. Could I have possibly screwed this up worse?"

"You're here with no backup—"

"Also my fault."

"No power, you can't even get an ambulance through. And really, how much help would your buddy have been if he were here? You'd have an extra pair of hands and eyes, but you still couldn't get the forensics done."

"And feeling bad about it doesn't solve the case. The storm is dying down. You'll have a whole crew of people crawling all over everything tomorrow, and you'll find the killer." Colin flipped his hands palm up. "You can only do what you can only do."

Fletcher nodded. "I'd feel a lot better if I had this resolved before everyone arrives. I mean, really, I am not looking good here."

"Little ego thing?" I teased.

"Big ego thing. But also, it's the 'my job is on the line' thing. Frankly, I like it here. I'd like to stay."

"Okay then. Let's figure this out."

Fletcher looked at the notes on the table. "Herbie? The sound guy?"

"He has a crush on Laura," Colin filled in. "And he may have worked with Marie Janeé."

"That's what we were going to tell you when we discovered Artie was missing. I guess it got lost in the sauce."

Fletcher was quiet for a minute, thinking. "Herbie is in the Green Room, packing up. Laura comes in, gets her dress, leaves. Sees Marie

Janeé in the hall and Marie Janeé is rude to her. So, Herbie overhears it and what? Stabs Marie Janeé in the hallway?" He shook his head. "It doesn't really fit."

"What if Laura lied to us?" I ventured. "What if she and Herbie killed Marie Janeé and then Herbie killed Josh while Laura had a solid alibi?"

"That makes more sense. That would make Laura a very good liar." He sounded doubtful. "Laura does not come across as someone who can lie that smoothly, much less actually murder someone. She seems so..."

"Fragile?" I asked.

"Yes. Not physically up to it," he responded.

"We've been taking Laura at her word about what happened during that whole time period." I looked at Fletcher.

"Sweet baby Jesus, I'm an idiot," Fletcher said softly. "I just felt so bad for her. That a-hole of a boyfriend and she's pregnant and sick..." He trailed off.

"Well, us too" Colin said.

"Hence, the need for an accomplice," I pointed out.

"Herbie." Fletcher's voice was flat.

"Hey, he wasn't top of our lists as a killer, either," I said.

"But, it makes sense. Herbie has a crush on Laura." Colin stood up and started acting it out. "Laura is verbally attacked by Marie Janeé. Herbie jumps in to defend her. Stab, stab, what do we do with the body, I don't know, hide it in the trunk, lock the door, go clean up and go to dinner."

"I don't know why he'd switch out the icicles, though," I said.

"He didn't. He just took the ornament string off to make it look like the prop icicle. Then he takes the clean prop icicle with him..." Fletcher shrugged.

"So, it looks like she was stabbed with the prop," I said.

"And then Herbie or Laura plants the string on Josh to pin Marie Janeé's murder on him," Colin brought it around full circle.

Fletcher's eyes narrowed, as he considered it. "Or, Herbie could have acted alone. He overhears the conversation, manages to get Marie Janeé into the Green Room. Kills her. Laura is none the wiser."

We were quiet for a few moments.

"One or both?" Colin asked.

"We won't know until we can prove at least one of them killed her. I'm not sure how we can do that."

"I have an idea," Fletcher said, and I saw him relax—just a bit—for the first time in two days.

Solving Murders... Not So Fun

"What are you going to do?" I asked.

"Arrest Laura. Put her in handcuffs and parade her down the hall. Your job, Kasey, is to make sure Herbie sees it."

"What do we say?"

"The truth. That I think Laura murdered Marie Janeé and then had an accomplice kill Josh."

"Who's the accomplice?" Colin asked.

"Well, it can't be me," I said. "I was with Laura when Josh was murdered."

"Me?" Colin's voice was about half an octave higher than normal.

"It's not like I'm really arresting you. Artie and I will cuff you, then go to Laura's room, cuff and collect her, then take her down to the event room for questioning. Artie will take you to another room and hide you away."

"Do you think Herbie will confess to save Laura?" I frowned, thinking that would take a lot of love.

"So far, everything he has done has been for Laura. Your job is to tell Herbie that Laura was the mastermind and she and Colin were having an affair."

"Will he buy that?"

"Thanks a lot!"

"Sorry. No offense, Colin."

Fletcher hesitated. "You'll need to sell it."

"Not making me feel any better," Colin said.

"I think Dan might be the better person for this," I said. "If he hears the commotion, he's going to come into the room and find a dozen reasons why Laura couldn't have had an affair with Colin. If you arrest Dan as her accomplice, Colin and I can both work that angle."

"I could mention that I had seen them out somewhere in Tampa or that I had seen them talking together a lot," Colin said.

"We're going to need Dan in here," Fletcher said. "I was trying to keep this to as few people as possible."

"Trust me, you're better off keeping Dan somewhere where his imagination can't run wild." I paused. "Colin, can you go across and knock softly on Dan's door and bring him back here?"

"Quiet as a mouse," Colin said.

I held open the door and flipped the latch around again, making sure it didn't make any noise when it shut. Dan's room was across from mine. Herbie's room was on the other side of Josh and Laura's, but the fisheye lens on the peephole gave anyone looking a fairly good view of the hallway. I was pretty sure Dan's room was out of viewing range, but maybe not out of sound range.

"Not having access to our cell phones is more of a pain in the neck than I would have admitted two days ago," I said.

"Just one more thing that went wrong this weekend," Fletcher sighed. "It's like the gods conspired against me."

"They didn't do too much for Marie Janeé or Josh, either, if it makes you feel any better."

"True."

Colin returned with Dan in tow. They shut the door completely and Dan looked around. "Where's Herbie?"

"Yeah, about Herbie," I started. We quickly brought Dan up to speed. He kept shaking his head in disbelief.

"Herbie? But we know Herbie..."

"We know Laura, too."

"Well, you said maybe she wasn't involved at all. Whoever killed Marie Janeé could have done it after Laura went down the hall."

"And who would have a reason to kill both Marie Janeé and Josh?" I asked him. "Think for a minute. Someone from VashTech or even Vitor might have killed Marie Janeé, but they would have no reason to kill Josh. It had to be one of us. Or maybe two of us."

"Unless *you* want to confess," Fletcher suggested.

Dan was confused. "Me? No, I would never... Oh. Yeah. Funny. Not. So, what do I do?"

"Go back to your room. In about twenty minutes, Artie and I will knock on your door. I'll place you under arrest, Artie will cuff you and bring you out in the hall. I want you to protest, but don't be too loud. I don't want a big commotion. Then I'll go knock on Laura's door and put her in custody. We all take the elevator down. I'll tell Artie that we need to separate you two. He'll take you to a private room so it will look like you're in custody. I'll take Laura to the event room for questioning."

"So, do you want Colin and me to pop our heads out of our doors to see what's going on?"

"Yes, with luck, Herbie will stick his head out, too. If not, you two need to knock on Herbie's door and tell him that Laura and Dan have been arrested."

"Not to sound like a wuss or anything, but you're asking Kasey and me to go into a room with a suspected murderer."

Fletcher winced. "That whole solve-a-murder thing isn't looking so fun right now, is it?"

"Not really," I said. "But there's two of us and Herbie has no reason to think we're a danger to him. I've had worse odds."

"Quick change of plan. Dan, once Artie parks you in a back office, I'll have him come back up to keep an eye on things. Maybe down the end of the hall." He shook his head. "No, that won't really work. Who has the room next to Herbie?"

Colin raised his hand. "I take it you can't use Josh and Laura's room."

"Best not to. Colin, give me your spare keycard. I'll have Artie go back into your room so if anything goes haywire, he's right there."

I subconsciously touched the back of my head where an attempted murderer had once hit me with the butt of a gun. In my limited experience, 'haywire' was usually painful. Plus, my faith in Artie's ability to handle more than a lost dog was approximately nil. I figured Colin and I were on our own. I'd let him know that once Fletcher was gone.

"What do you want to happen on our side? I mean, I doubt if Herbie will confess anything to us," Colin said.

"Let him know that I'm most likely questioning Laura in the event room. If he wants to clear Laura's name, he needs to get to me."

"You're setting yourself up," I said.

"Your job is to get him to take action. Ideally, he will come after me, try to free Laura or he'll come confess to me to clear Laura's name. Either way, I want him to come to me."

"What if he doesn't do anything?" Dan asked.

"If Laura was in on it, she may reveal that Herbie was her accomplice. But, as we've said, there is an off-chance that she wasn't in on it."

"I would like that to be true," Dan said.

Colin and I nodded silently.

"And if Laura wasn't in on it and Herbie doesn't confess?"

"In that case, I'm screwed because two people are dead and I'm coming up empty."

"He just gets away with it?"

"Until the forensics team comes up with some evidence."

The plan felt unsubstantial and I wondered if Fletcher felt as hopeless about it as I did. But really, what else could he do? The least we could do was help him in any way we could.

I tried to inject some enthusiasm into my voice. "Okay, then, let's do this. I think you're right. Herbie has done everything because he loves Laura. He's not going to let her take the rap alone."

Fletcher looked relieved. "I'm going to go down and check on Artie. If he can't do it, I'll get the night manager or someone who looks official. It's not like we're really arresting Dan, so all we need is an extra set of cuffs. I'll be back up in about twenty minutes. Dan, wait five minutes here and then go back to your room. Quietly."

"Sure."

He let himself out, closing the door against the latch gently and moving quietly down the corridor. He must have taken the stairs because I didn't hear the elevator ding.

Dan looked at us, wide-eyed. "What do you think Herbie is going to do when Laura is arrested?"

I shifted uncomfortably. "The best option is we convince him that Laura needs saving and get him to go down to the event room. Second best is that he confesses to us, in which case, Colin" I looked directly at him, "and I do our best to pretend to be on his side, while telling him he needs to go confess to Fletcher."

"While not triggering him to murder both of us," Colin commented.

"Well, yeah, that. But really, why would he?"

"Because he just confessed committing a double murder to us?"

"Good point. Let's hope our acting ability is better than what we used for this show."

"Hey, it's not easy to be a happy *little* elf when you're six foot four," Dan said.

"Or when someone is groping you," I came back.

"Kind of sad when playing Santa's elves is one of your better roles," Colin observed. "At least we'll get to say our best scenes never get an audience."

"We'll have to do it for our art," I said.

"Oh yeah, this is art all right." Dan stood up. "Time to go back to my room and await my arrest. I'm glad my mom won't see this."

"And it's good practice in case you ever get cast as the bad guy in a cop show." I had learned to frame everything in terms of acting jobs to Dan, otherwise he got overwhelmed. I know every actor thinks it, but I figured I'd probably make a good director. Or day care worker.

I watched Dan go back to his room through the inch crack in the door. Colin and I waited another five minutes, mostly in tense silence. Colin went back to his room and I was left to wait alone.

Shiver Me Timbers

Fletcher knew how to create some drama. He and Artie knocked on Laura's and Dan's doors simultaneously. The knocks were loud enough to wake people up and to bring more than a few eyeballs to the peepholes.

"Laura Myers. Open up. Police."

Artie identified himself as hotel security and Dan opened his door almost immediately. I could hear Artie saying something and Dan protesting. Laura took more time to come to the door. When she opened it, Fletcher placed her under arrest and put her in handcuffs. There was no need to worry about people coming to the doors to have a look; doors were cracking open all down the hall.

Fletcher and Artie escorted Laura and Dan to the elevators. The rest of us were left gaping at each other. I noticed the VashTech people were not looking at us kindly.

Colin looked at Herbie and then me. "You guys, come in my room. We need to talk!"

"No kidding," I said, playing along. I had my keycard in my pocket. Herbie ducked back into his room and came out seconds later.

Colin's room had file folders stacked on the table and his laptop was open on one of the beds. Herbie and I took seats at the table.

"What the hell just happened?" I asked.

Herbie shook his head. "I don't know. They're arresting Laura for the murders? She was with Fletcher when Josh was killed."

Colin saw his opportunity. "Which might explain why they arrested Dan, too. He could have killed Josh to give Laura some cover."

"His shoes were wet!" I said, as if I had just thought of it.

"And there was water under Josh's body," Colin added.

"But Fletcher said the shoe size was wrong," Herbie protested.

"Maybe he wanted Dan to think he was in the clear?"

"Sneaky. Maybe Fletcher has more on the ball than we thought," Colin said.

"I can't believe Laura would kill anyone." He stood up, looking for some room to pace and really didn't have it.

"I need a drink." Colin went over to the counter area and pulled out his bottle of bourbon. "Anyone else?"

I wasn't up for bourbon on top of scotch. "No. I'm so upset, I think I'm going to throw up."

"I've seen enough throwing up for one night," Herbie said. He walked over and picked up one of the glasses. "Have any Coke to go with that bourbon?"

Colin reached into the mini fridge and fixed the drink. "No ice, sorry."

"I need the bourbon more than the ice." Herbie took a big gulp and then looked around. "It doesn't make sense. Why would Dan kill Josh?"

Colin looked around the room, pretending to have difficulty meeting our eyes.

"Do you have something to tell us?" I asked.

"I think Laura and Dan had a thing," he said.

"A thing?"

"Yeah, I saw them out once in Tampa. They were having lunch and they looked a little friendlier than Josh would have liked."

"Laura and Dan?" Herbie scoffed.

"Face it, Dan is more than good-looking," I said.

"Yeah, but Laura is older than he is," Herbie protested.

"Dan goes out with older women all the time," Colin pointed out. "Maybe the baby is his."

Herbie blanched. "That's disgusting."

"Better than carrying on Josh's genes," I said. "Do you think Dan helped her kill Marie Janeé or do you think she did it on her own?"

"How can you even think that? Laura doesn't have it in her to kill anyone."

"Herbie, she's pregnant, she feels awful. Her hormones are all over the place. Josh tells her that she's a second-rate Marie Janeé and then Marie Janeé says those awful things to her. I mean, I would have at least taken a swing at her if she had said those things to me. Maybe it all just became too much and Laura lost it. Kind of an accident."

"What about the blood on Laura's dress? There was no blood on the dress!"

"We can't find the dress she was wearing. Or couldn't. Maybe Fletcher found it and that was the final bit of evidence he needed to arrest her."

"This is just wrong," Herbie muttered.

"Look, Fletcher must have found some evidence that pointed to Laura and then to Dan. I'm not real happy that we've been spending time with a murderer."

I shot a look at Colin. His comment was a little too close to the bone.

"What do you think Fletcher is doing to them now?" I asked, hoping to divert Herbie's attention away from that last bit.

"Probably questioning them. I think he'll start with Laura."

Colin's room phone rang. We all jumped.

"The phones work?" I asked rhetorically.

"Maybe the power is back on?"

"It's an internal system," Herbie said. "They never really stopped working. The server is being run off a generator."

Colin picked up the phone.

"Hello. Yes, sir."

He looked over at us and mouthed "Fletcher."

"Clarify where Dan was when Marie Janeé was killed? Well, actually, he didn't come up to the room *with* me. He said he was stopping by the gift shop to get something. But we both showed up at the dining room about the same time. False information? No!" There was a pause. "Well, yeah, but um, things kind of got jumbled up." Another pause. "Sorry. I didn't think."

We heard a loud click.

Colin sank down on the bed. "Crap. He's thinking about arresting me for false information. I was so freaked out about finding Marie Janeé, I forgot that Dan didn't come up to the rooms with me." He looked at us and I felt sorry for him, even though I knew he was acting.

"Dan didn't quite get all his makeup off that night. He must have rushed through it. Remember?" I looked at Herbie. "He still had traces of the red circles on his cheeks."

"He must have doubled back to the Green Room to meet up with Laura for a little hanky-panky," Colin said.

Herbie stood up. "I was still in the Green Room. I didn't see Dan double back. Besides, there's no way Laura was having an affair with Dan. I'm not going to sit here and listen to this. It's all speculation."

"I guess," I said slowly. "But if this is where the evidence leads, Laura is going to have her baby in jail. Unless Dan admits to killing both Marie Janeé and Josh."

"That would clear Laura," Colin said. "Do you think Dan loves her that much?"

"That would take a lot of love. I don't know too many people who would do that. At this point, it's probably every man for himself. He'll rat Laura out for murdering Marie Janeé and Laura will give up her accomplice in a New York second."

Herbie put his glass down on bureau. "I've got to go."

"I guess we'll see you in the morning," I said.

Colin closed the door behind him and looked at me, his eyes wide. "Oh my God, that was insane."

"Look through the peephole. Did he go back to his room?"

We crowded at the door for a minute.

"He's coming out," Colin whispered. "He's wearing a jacket so he must be... no, he's heading back this way."

"What?"

We jumped back from the door and jumped again when Herbie knocked. I scurried back to my seat at the table. Colin waited a few seconds before opening the door.

"Hey man. Are you okay?"

"No, not at all. I want to go down and see Laura. Fletcher has to know that she didn't do it."

"Okay," I said, not sure where this was leading.

"Will you guys come with me?" He held up a cloth bag. "I've got juice and some snacks for Laura. Saltines." He sounded so lost.

"Of course, we'll go down with you," Colin said. "But I'm sure Fletcher is making sure she has water and whatever she needs. He knows she's pregnant."

"I just have to check on her."

I stood up and we trooped out of the room. It was past midnight and after the earlier ruckus, the corridor was strangely silent. We waited for the elevator, not speaking. Herbie shifted back and forth from one foot to the other, looking at the ground. The elevator doors opened up and we started the ride down.

"I hope this is all a big mistake," I started, hoping to keep Herbie calm.

"You bet it is," Herbie said. "How could anyone suspect Laura of killing anyone?"

"Do you think Dan did it?" Colin asked.

"Maybe." Herbie's eyes darted down to the side. Was he thinking of ways to frame Dan for this?

We walked through the lobby to the event room. The door was halfway open. Fletcher must have realized it wouldn't look good to be alone with a suspect. I popped my head in.

"Deputy? We just wanted to check on Laura."

"She's fine. But I don't want to be interrupted."

Herbie pushed me through the door and then Colin. He came in behind us and closed the door.

"What the hell, Herbie?" Colin said.

He held up the bag and what looked like a remote control. "Go stand over there by the deputy."

"Is that a—"

"MOVE!"

Colin and I scurried across the room. Fletcher was standing with his hand on his holster.

"Let's all calm down here."

"Yes, let's. Because these things are very fragile and I'm kind of new to bomb making." He stepped closer to us. "Deputy Fletcher, I need you to hand your weapon to Laura."

"Herbie, what are you doing? This is not going to work!" Laura held the gun gingerly, and I hoped that Fletcher didn't have a round chambered.

Fletcher was acquiescent. "Okay, Laura has the gun. We don't want anyone to get hurt here, Herbie. Why don't you just put down the—"

"NO! I'm giving the orders. We're getting off this island now."

"There's no way to get off the island. The ferry doesn't start up until tomorrow at the earliest."

"The storm has died down. There's a police boat docked in the marina. I assume you know how to use it."

Fletcher nodded. "I can handle the boat, but the water is still too rough and it's pitch black out there."

"Good thing you have navigation equipment onboard. Let's get going."

"All of us?" I asked.

"I'm not going to hurt you guys. But I need you for insurance. Fletcher gets Laura and me to the other side, you all head back, safe as can be. All I want is a head start."

"We're going to need coats. It's cold and wet out there," I said, trying to delay things.

"There'll be blankets on the boat. You'll have to be uncomfortable for an hour or so. Take the corridor down towards the pool. We'll go out that way."

I looked at Fletcher and he nodded. Colin and I walked together, Fletcher and Laura behind us with Herbie bringing up the rear.

"Why didn't Fletcher do something?" Colin asked.

"If Herbie really does have a bomb, Fletcher doesn't want him setting it off in a hotel with a hundred or more people in it."

"We're the sacrificial lambs?"

"Acceptable losses. He's including himself with us."

We went out the pool deck door and worked our way around to the path leading down to the marina. It was relatively cold, probably in the 40s and I started shivering immediately. I hate the cold. The wind was still whipping in and it brought waves of rain with it, but not nearly as heavy as the rain had been last night. Nevertheless, we were soaked immediately.

"We're going to catch pneumonia," I said.

"We'll be lucky to just catch pneumonia," Colin whispered back.

"Stop talking, you two," Herbie called out.

"Sorry, Herbie. Just bitching about the cold."

"Boat has a cabin. You'll be fine."

I glanced back. Laura had dropped back to walk with Herbie. She didn't bother to whisper.

"Herbie, this is crazy. I didn't kill anyone. You don't have to do this."

Fletcher's voice was clear. "He knows you didn't kill anyone, Laura. So do I. Herbie, you want to fill Laura in?"

"I did it for you, Laura."

"Did what?" She stopped as realization hit her and Herbie grabbed her arm and pulled her along.

"Oh, I'm going to be sick."

"Hold it together, Laura," I tossed over my shoulder. "Herbie doesn't want to hurt anyone, especially you. It's going to be fine."

Colin looked over at me.

"I hope," I said softly.

"Did Marie Janeé even recognize you, Herbie? Is that how you got her into the Green Room?" I asked.

"Of course she didn't recognize me. I worked shows with her for over a year. Even then, Marie Janeé was a snot. I wasn't important enough for her to notice. But she did remember the cape from *Dracula*. All I had to do was remind her I had worked those shows. I said she was the only decent actor in the troupe. I knew she'd like that. She walked right over to me, pretending she remembered me. As if. No one remembers me. I raised up my arms like Dracula and swept her right into the room, just like we did in the show. She didn't even scream. She giggled." He gave a short laugh and I felt the hair on my neck stand up.

"She even did the line, just like in the show."

"He was wearing the cape," Colin whispered to me. "No blood on him."

"And you stabbed her with the prop icicle," Fletcher said, trying to keep Herbie talking. Colin started to react and I squeezed his hand.

"No. You really aren't too bright, are you?" Herbie's voice had more than an edge of arrogance. "I grabbed an ornament from the tree. Easy peasy. When I went to hide the body, there was the icicle sitting on top. Identical. Identical icicle. At first glance, at least."

I could hear Laura crying softly. I thought about how easy it would be for Herbie to overpower Marie Janeé. He was used to lifting and carrying all his equipment. She was probably a hundred pounds soaking wet. Easy peasy indeed.

We were down to the pier area and I hesitated, not sure where the police boat was tied up.

"Aisle C, at the end," Fletcher said. "Anyone here have any boating experience?"

"I don't suppose getting drunk on a gambling cruise counts," Colin said.

"I've done a little sailing," I offered. Very little, but I could untie a line. "Herbie? How about you?"

"I've got my hands full," he smirked.

"More so when Laura starts puking again," I muttered to Colin.

The police boat was bobbing in its dock. The waves were still pretty rough, especially for the Gulf, and water was slopping over the piers. It made the going slippery. I tried not to think about what the salt water was doing to my shoes.

"Everyone get on board. Fletcher, you get this thing started."

"Kasey, I need you to handle the dock lines. That means it's going to be a little harder for you to get on the boat. I'll hold it as close to the pier as I can, but we're bouncing all over the place here."

Fletcher had just thrown me a get out of jail free card. I looked at him and nodded. I got it. He planned to leave me at the dock. One less hostage.

"Got it."

"Start with the stern line."

I gave him a puzzled look. Even I knew that you wanted the engines turning before you started untying lines. He looked me full in the eyes and nodded.

Fletcher scrambled aboard and turned to help Laura and then Colin. I took the opportunity to unwrap the stern line from the cleat, leaving one loop around it and held it tight. I felt like my arms were going to get pulled out of their sockets. Fletcher had turned to help Herbie into the boat.

Herbie slung the cloth bag over his shoulder and started to step onto the boat. As he did, I dropped the line and kicked the stern away from the pier. His raised-up foot hit air. Fletcher knocked him into the water. We waited for an explosion that didn't come.

Herbie bobbed up, arms flailing. He no longer had the remote control in his hand. He'd also lost the bag. I hoped the force of the waves wouldn't set off the bomb. Herbie screamed before he went under the waves again and I looked around for a life ring or a boat hook. Fletcher tossed a life ring into the water, but Herbie couldn't see it.

I ran the few steps to the end of the pier to grab another life ring. When Herbie surfaced again, I called to him to get his attention then threw the ring. He flailed his way to it and held on for dear life. I started pulling on the line, dragging him in. I searched for a ladder, but couldn't see one. No way could I pull Herbie onto the pier. He was going to have to hang on. I walked the line around to the end of the pier and cleated it off, giving Fletcher room to bring the boat back in.

"Hang on!"

"Get me up, get me up!"

"I can't lift you. I'm going to need help. Hold tight."

I could feel the pier heave every time the waves pushed the boat. The bowline was still attached, but the weight of the boat was straining the line, the cleat, and it felt like the pier itself.

The boat had swung out almost its full length. Fletcher started the engine and was goosing it to get closer to the pier. Colin pulled the dragging stern line into the boat and as they drew near, tried to toss it to me. I missed. He pulled it in, then tossed it again and I grabbed at it clumsily, clamping the line between my arms, before getting my hands on it. The weight of the boat against the line was pulling at me. I managed to loop it around the cleat to take some of the pressure off me before I got pulled into the water. The boat came closer which gave me the slack I needed to tighten the line and tie it down.

Fletcher put the boat in neutral and came out of the small cabin.

"Laura, there are blankets in the cabin in the locker. Grab them, but stay aboard until we can get you off safely. Colin, I'm going to need you."

I helped Colin and Fletcher scramble off the boat. We went down to where I had left Herbie. He was still yelling.

The two guys lay down flat on the pier and as it shifted down, they grabbed Herbie and hauled him up. He lay on the dock, breathing hard and shivering.

Good, I thought. *If I have to be cold, you should be freezing.*

God Bless Us Everyone

"With Josh dead, and Herbie arrested, what are we going to do?"
Dan asked.

"What do you mean?"

"We have six gigs booked for this show between now and Christmas, plus the wedding show in January."

"I guess we cancel them. Do you think they're paid for already? They might need refunds."

We looked at Laura.

"Josh has deposits for the shows. But that money is pretty much spent."

"And we need a new sound guy," Dan said.

"Did we even get paid for this show?" Colin asked.

Laura held up the check from VashTech. It was made out to the company for $1,500.

"Fifteen hundred dollars?" Colin looked at the check disbelievingly.

"Holy crap. He was paying us $200..." Dan said.

"Yeah. We did the work and he got most of the money." Colin was not happy.

"That's just half of it. He gets fifty percent when he takes the booking." I looked at Laura.

"Well, if it makes you feel any better, I was getting the same as you. Josh said he had to keep the company running." Laura said.

"Should we give something to Josh's family?" I asked.

"Does he even have a family? I think he was raised by wolves." Colin was definitely pissed.

"He doesn't, actually. Parents are dead. He was an only child." She looked sad.

I thought about what it must have been like to be Josh, having no one and still driving everyone away.

"Five of us. Three hundred each," Dan said.

"Four. I don't think Herbie should get a cut. All things considered," Colin pointed out.

"That works for me," Dan said, then he felt bad. "Well, technically, he did work the show. And he's going to need money for lawyers. And bail."

I looked at Colin and Dan. "So, five ways, then. We good?"
They nodded.

"Give me a couple of days to get this deposited and write out new checks," Laura said. "I can get checks to you guys at Friday's show."

"We're going to need a new sound guy by then," Dan said.

"I know a guy, another prof at the university. He does DJ work. Let me see if he's available." Colin started to take out his phone and realized we didn't have signal on the ferry. He looked at Laura. "I'll let you know as soon as I know."

She nodded. "Hey, listen. I'm sorry, but you're going to need a new stage manager. And director. And producer. I'm not staying."

We looked at her. "Laura, you're in charge of the company now. We kind of need you."

"I'll stay for the next couple of weeks, finish the Christmas shows. But, I was going back home for the holidays. I think I will just stay there. If I'm going to have this baby, I'm going to need some support."

"Of course you will. Family is best," I said.

She looked at us. "That means I need someone to take over the company."

Colin said, "I am busy enough with my day job."

"I don't know anything about running a business. I just want to act. What about you, Kasey?" Dan looked at me.

"Me? I, uh, I don't know." I looked at them. "Can I think about it?"

"Really, Kasey, it's a going concern that you can just step into," Laura pointed out. "It doesn't make a lot of money, but it does turn a profit."

"C'mon, Kasey. You'd be great at this," Dan cajoled.

"I know as much about running a business as Dan does."

Laura shook her head. "Not true. You've been booking yourself as a comic. It wouldn't be so hard to book the show. And maybe create more bookings for yourself. Maybe offer comedy shows, too."

That put a new spin on things. I could book myself and other comics that I knew. It was a big step forward.

"I'm going to need some help to get things figured out," I said.

I could see the relief on Laura's face. "I can show you the booking calendar and all the marketing materials we use. It's super simple. We get a 50% deposit upfront, and basically pay the cast out of the other 50%. You know the wedding show and that cast is easy. Occasionally you have to break in a new cast member. You can do this."

I took a deep breath and nodded. "You're going to need to hold my hand for the first few shows."

"First order of business is the new sound guy," Laura looked at Colin. "I've got the music and I can run him through the cues."

"I know Herbie's set up," Colin said. "I'll run through it with my buddy. Luckily, this show is mostly sound effects then Christmas carols. The wedding show is more complex, but we have time."

I nodded. "Well, let's give it a try."

The guys high-fived me. I exhaled. "So, okay. I guess Laura and I will figure out the business paperwork." I looked at her. "If you want, I can call the other company members and let them know what's going on."

I wasn't looking forward to that, but it would have been torture for Laura. I wondered vaguely if anyone would have a problem with me taking over the troupe, but really, with Laura, Dan and Colin already in my camp, it was a done deal.

There would be time to figure out if there were any deposits and hopefully have a smooth transition. I looked out at the mainland as we drew closer. I was now a director. And a producer. Is that how it worked? You just said you were and you were? I felt a moment of panic. Colin leaned into me.

"You'll be fine," he whispered.

Once we got to the mainland, we loaded the hat boxes into my car. I hugged the guys and took a last look at the island. I was pretty sure I wouldn't schedule any future shows there. But then again, what were the odds of that repeating?

I turned to get into my car as another car pulled in fast, scattering gravel. Two people in the front seat. Wait. No. One person. One monkey. Thankfully, the monkey wasn't driving.

"Is that the ferry to Nokosi Island?"

"Yep. Just got in."

"Thank God. Jax and I were supposed to do a show last night for VashTech corporation, but we couldn't get there. I need to apologize to the lady who booked us. I hope they don't want their deposit back."

"The Incredible Jax?"

"You know him?"

"We've met. California? Last year?"

"Oh, yeah. Hi. Small world."

I looked at Jax. He was grinning at me. "Small world indeed."

"Anyway, I hope the client will understand."

"Don't worry about it. And I don't think you need to worry about the deposit either."

"Good thing, because we spent part of it on a hotel here."

I had a thought. "Give me your business card. I'll talk to Edward about you. Explain the situation."

"Oh, I talked to a woman. A Marie Janet or something."

"Yeah. Um, she's no longer with the company." I took his card. Who knew, maybe I could book The Incredible Jax in somewhere.

"So, should I bother going out there?"

"Probably not. They're cutting their retreat short. They'll all be leaving in a few hours. We got the first boat out."

"I guess I wasted money staying at a hotel, but I thought I could salvage something of the weekend."

"You didn't miss a thing."

Keep In Touch

Want to know when the next Kasey McCormick Mystery is coming out? Or just like free, fun, bookish stuff?

Visit my website: BonnieCavaliere.com and sign on for access to my monthly newsletter and the Freebie Library. (Lots of fun freebies!)

See you soon!

Bonnie

While you're here...

Other books in the Kasey McCormick Series:

Fez Up (Get it for free on my website!)

The Girl in the Pork Pie Hat

Top Hats and Treachery